T0355061

Is School Really Out For The Summer?

Is School Really Out For The Summer?

Abbreviated Musings
of a High School
Principal

Jim Sarto

ARCHWAY
PUBLISHING

Archway Publishing books may be ordered through booksellers or by contacting:

Archway Publishing
1663 Liberty Drive
Bloomington, IN 47403
www.archwaypublishing.com
844-669-3957

ISBN: 978-1-6657-6671-5 (sc)
ISBN: 978-1-6657-6673-9 (hc)
ISBN: 978-1-6657-6672-2 (e)

Library of Congress Control Number: 2024920940

Print information available on the last page.

Archway Publishing rev. date: 11/23/2024

To the countless phenomenal educators who offer their time, effort, and dedication, twenty-four/seven, twelve months a year, for our youth. For them, school does not end at the three o'clock bell, on Fridays, or during the summer months. Each of them has days that no one but an educator would believe. At one point or another, every one of them has said, "I could write a book!"

This one is mine. And this one's for you!

Don't take life, or this book, too seriously.
Life's too short ... and so is this book.

—Dr. Joseph Strat

I've eaten at thousands of restaurants. I could easily open a restaurant.

I've shopped for clothes all my life. I could, without a doubt, open a clothing store.

I've gone to school pre-K through grade 12 plus ... I absolutely could run a school. How hard could it be? Maybe I'll run for the board of education!

CONTENTS

ACKNOWLEDGMENTS

A special thank-you to my wife, Karen, my kids, Tyler, Matthew, Grace, and William, and the rest of my relatives who have tolerated having an educator in the family. I couldn't have done it without 'em!

CHAPTER 1

Graduation Night

June 20

Once again, it was graduation night at Avenue Ridge High School. The township also offered a middle school for grades 6 to 8 and three elementary schools for pre-K to fifth grade. All were slightly below "Ave Ridge."

It was 5:58 p.m. on the visitors' side of the fifty-yard line at our high school football stadium. Everyone took their place as we got ready to go. Mr. Bland, one of our senior guidance counselors, walked by each senior individually, holding up an empty coffee cup for them to spit their wads of gum into.

The superintendent, administration, and I (the principal) would lead the commencement down the fifty-yard line, followed by the board of education members, faculty, staff, and of course, the graduating seniors.

"Let's rock and roll!" I shouted as the clock struck 6:00 p.m. sharp. The parade down the fifty-yard line was not quite in step as the seniors began to forget everything that was covered during the past two days of practice.

The band, minus the senior band members (a.k.a. the better

1

players), cranked out their rendition of "Pomp and Circumstance," which would make Sir Edward Elgar cringe.

The crowd in the home bleachers rose, chanting, "We are Ave Ridge! We are Ave Ridge!" while simultaneously stomping on the aluminum floorboards. This was immediately followed by the shouting out of student names, slang phrases, undiscernible noises, and of course an air horn or two.

It was going to be another "classy" graduation.

The reality was the crowd wanted to see their children get their diplomas, take a few pics, then run off the field and into their futures. No one wanted to hear my lengthy speech so I aimed for under two minutes and a total graduation ceremony of just under an hour. Primo!

The seniors reached their seats that stretched from forty-yard line to forty-yard line, forgetting which rows they were assigned. Once in place, they focused on the valedictorian to seat them. She waved her hands up then down just like in practice, but instead of sitting in unison, the class went down in a broken wave.

As the students and staff began to bake on the field under a cloudless sky, the choral director arranged the fifteen members of the vocal ensemble to belt out a nameless tune to over two thousand stadium guests, making use of a marginal sound system designed for indoor classroom use only. The audience saw what they could only guess was the chorus miming a song, so this was the perfect opportunity for our dignified scholars to blow up beach balls and inflatable dolls and volley them among the graduating class.

The staff, sitting at key points around the senior class, made a valiant attempt at retrieving the inflated projectiles.

As I said, "Classy!"

There was the traditional pledge to the flag and the singing of our national anthem.

The salutatorian then offered opening remarks while family

members in the stands hollered their children's names, whistled, and blew air horns at random.

The senior class president's speech was next. As he read the opening line, it was evident he'd switched from the approved speech to go rogue.

"I had a prepared speech, but I thought I would go with my gut," he began. "Let me tell you a little about my classmates."

The superintendent gave me side-eye as I sank slightly into my chair.

He ended with "I'll see you losers on the other side!"

The senior class whooped, cheered, and hollered. So did the entirety of the grandstands.

When sending home graduation invitations each year, I liked to include the traditional guest expectations letter.

- Please be courteous to others in the home stands.
- Please hold your applause until all the graduates have received their diplomas.
- Please do not shout out or applaud individual seniors. Others may not be fortunate enough to have as many friends and/or relatives in attendance.
- Absolutely *no air horns!*

If your assistant principal takes seriously the last line of his contract (and all other duties assigned by the principal), he will have replaced the liquid in your water bottles with a premium vodka. When one of the guest expectations is not being followed, time for a shot! *Perhaps next year,* I thought.

(PS: In the event your assistant principal is really on the ball, an Uber for the ride home is highly recommended.)

As I walked up to the podium, the sounds of unruly parents verbally assaulting one another across the grandstands could be heard. Our hired security detail could be seen in the parking lot sharing coffee with the EMTs, oblivious to their surroundings.

The crowd settled as I began my speech, which ended with the traditional "Dr. Fieldman, I certify that these students have fulfilled all the requirements set forth by the state to graduate. May I introduce to you our graduating senior class?"

The seniors stood up proudly. Not in unison as practiced, but at least most of them were listening.

The graduates sat down (not together) as the superintendent began her speech.

I walked back to my seat, locking eyes with my assistant principal, Mr. Minor. No words needed to be spoken.

To ease the tension, Mr. Minor whispered, "Nice speech. In record time at one minute, forty-five seconds!"

As Superintendent Fieldman concluded her speech, the time had arrived to award the diplomas to the senior class. The valedictorian and salutatorian took to the podium to individually announce the graduates' names as they slow-walked their way on and off the portable stage. They were joined by the superintendent of schools, along with the only two sober board members in attendance. The board members were, of course, dressed as if they were attending their junior prom.

I remained seated in the front row along with Mr. Minor as the senior names were announced. We shared a knowing glance when certain names were called. Would these fine graduates be millionaires or in jail by the time they were twenty-five? Would their helicopter parents follow them to college? The workforce? The military? Would next year's crop be as "unique" as this class? Would I win the lottery tonight, and …?

It was obvious one of our more rebellious female students had not followed the dress code associated with wearing a graduation gown. She confidently marched across the stage to accept her diploma with the setting sun making her white gown transparent, displaying her uncovered endowment proudly.

The class cheered! The spectators cheered! The board attorney and I pretended to be looking at our iPhones. The superintendent took mental notes while shaking her head.

Once the last graduates received their diplomas and made their way back to their seats, Superintendent Fieldman stopped in front of my seat to shake my hand. Smiling, she whispered to me, "We'll talk later!" then released my hand.

The class valedictorian was next to speak. Her speech was well thought out, timely, articulate, and appreciative. A generous and respectful round of applause followed as the crowd half listened.

It was now time for the singing of the school alma mater. The choral director took his place in front of the graduates to lead them in singing. This was always a tearjerker at any graduation. When sung at its best, it was usually still unrecognizable. Most seniors had no idea there even was an alma mater until the second graduation practice.

Ah, tradition! I thought as a smattering of applause followed.

The senior class president smiled in the direction of his classmates and moved his tassel from right to left. The senior class followed suit as loud cheers erupted from the entire stadium.

They were now graduates!

"Just under an hour," Mr. Minor whispered to me. "Nice job!"

With the band performing what I could only imagine was Beethoven's "Ode to Joy," the senior class threw their caps in the air and then began to leave in single file to the recessional. This lasted for about ten seconds before they scattered like golden retriever puppies in all directions.

For the next few minutes, students and staff could be seen embracing one another (some just a little longer than others), kissing, and holding hands, making the alternate board attorney covering for this event cringe and shake her head. Our regular attorney never would have caught it. A few faculty members also took advantage of this time to slip their personal business cards to select students. The board attorney ran to her car, again shaking her head, while staring directly at the ground. We never saw her again.

My advice to the staff was that during this "grip and grin" cameras would be flashing and taking audio/video of *everything*. "Smile, grip and grin, and say little that could be recorded and used against you in a court of law. Or even worse, on social media!"

It is interesting to note that the parents who wanted you taken to court and/or fired for the last four years were the first ones who came up to thank you and ask to have a picture taken with their seniors. "Grip and grin!"

As the graduates and their families left the stadium, the teachers and staff had already begun their celebratory pub crawl, aware that their last official day of the school year was tomorrow, beginning at 7:00 a.m.

At the entrance to the parking lot, I could see a barricade of band parents selling 50/50 tickets to help raise funds for the Ave Ridge marching band to compete in the Antarctica: Frozen in Time competition next spring. Now that was dedication!

A few untenured staff shouted to me as I worked my way back to the office, "Are you gonna join us, Principal Strat?"

"Not this time," I said as I waved them on.

CHAPTER 2

Tomorrow's the Last Day of School!
(I Want Another Fifth-Grade Summer)

June 16, 1964

"Joey! Joey Strat!" my mother called out the front door. "Time for dinner!"

I nodded to my friends, headed up the driveway on my red Schwinn Sting-Ray bike, and parked it against the old oak tree by the back door.

My family took their usual spots at the dining room table while not saying much, just being hungry. Dad always sat at the head of the table with the window directly behind him and the shade down. Mom sat on the other end by the kitchen. I always sat to Dad's left with my kid brother Bud between me and Mom. My older brother TJ sat across from me with my sister Dexie across from Bud and next to Mom.

It was a Tuesday night so that meant Swanson TV dinners. As I peeled back the tin foil covering the chicken, peas, and mashed potatoes, I could hear "All My Loving" by the Beatles playing on the RCA Hi-Fi that was sitting proudly by the Zenith black-and-white television in the living room. My mother and father were big fans. My mother was in love with Paul McCartney. My father thought John Lennon had all the talent. They were all right, I guess. But they couldn't hold a candle to Herman's Hermits.

Tomorrow would be my last day of school as a fifth grader. I didn't know why we even bothered to go in. It was only for two hours and all of our books and supplies had already been collected. I think the principal just did it for spite.

When dinner was over, my brothers and sister gathered in the living room for some TV time before going to bed. My mom and dad usually took this time to have a glass of wine around the dining table to catch up on the events of the day. Their go-to was the gallon jug of Gallo port. They joined us in the living room a short time later.

When it was nine o'clock, my mom shouted, "Bedtime!"

Since tomorrow was the last day of school, we went upstairs to our rooms to rush the start of the summer. I looked out my bedroom window at the neighborhood and saw the upstairs lights going out one after another at my friend's houses. Although it was dark, I could see the light at the end of the tunnel.

I opened the windows as wide as they would go and turned on my floor fan. The nights were getting hotter, which was a sure sign summer was around the corner. I took the blanket off the bed and slipped under the cover sheet. It took a little while to fall sleep, but when I did, it was a deep sleep.

CHAPTER 3

The Last Day of School!

June 21

I arrived early to school, as usual, carried in my Dunkin' coffee, and greeted the three veteran staff members I could always count on to be in the building at the crack of dawn. The remainder of the staff crawled in wondering if anyone would approach them prior to sobering up. Thirty-five percent of the students who made the attempt to come in for the last day of school arrived in spurts, minus the senior class. Well, that's not entirely true. A handful of graduates just had to make an appearance as "alumni."

In the main hallway, a random student groaned, *"Is today really necessary?"*

Other students and staff gave understanding glances and nods.

"Hey, the day counts," I said to myself.

In the back of my mind, I thought, *If I have an evacuation drill then lock all the doors, I could take an early lunch.*

For the next four hours, every living thing in the building watched the clock move in slow motion. The teachers made a valiant effort to keep the students in their classrooms, occupied and amused. This, of course, worked out as well as you think it would.

At the final bell, students raced to the exits while fighting their way past the occasional staff members trying desperately to get to their cars first.

My head custodian, Iggy, seeing the condition of the hallways, classrooms, and open lockers, began to visibly weep. The staff members who remembered they should sign out gathered in the main office. A few submitted their keys and checkout lists that were due last week. Others wished the office staff and my team a restful summer then bolted to the door.

Dr. Barium burst into the office with a beaming smile and shouted, "Finally the last day!"

Dr. Barium, a man about fifty-six years of age, had been our AP physics teacher and department supervisor for the past eighteen years. He was a pale gentleman with silvery gray hair. Bypassing the others, he shook my hand with both of his and exclaimed, "I'm moving to Paris to pursue my passion as an artist!"

A little taken back, I forced a grin and offered congratulations. "Are you serious?" I said, hoping this was a joke. "You will be back in September, right?"

"Nope! And absolutely serious!" he said. "Maybe I should have told you sooner, but I just came to this revelation over the weekend. Life's too short so ... What the heck!"

I said, "Why don't we go into my office and—"

"Would love to, but gotta run. I'll call you. Bye, everyone. Miss me!" he said as he ran off.

Stepping up quickly behind him was my English teacher of one whole year who shyly said, "Schoolkids and their entitled parents just aren't my thing. Sorry." She scurried off, leaving a handwritten resignation letter on the counter before I could say a word.

Next Mr. Trey, a forty-one-year fixture at the school as an

art and photography teacher, gingerly placed his boxes on the countertop then shook my hand. Today began his retirement.

His retirement dinner last Thursday evening was well attended by past students, staff, and community members. There were music, dancing, wonderful food, drinks, and a prepared speech by the guest of honor that brought a standing ovation ... Epic!

On this last day, during this heartfelt moment, I said, "Thank you for your dedication and years of service. Enjoy your well-deserved retirement, and don't be a stranger!"

Mr. Trey gave one final wave and grabbed the boxes on the counter. One slipped out of his hands and hit the floor, spilling out the contents. Everyone in the office immediately helped gather them up. A hush went over the crowd as they saw four decades worth of pictures of Mr. Trey's students—let's just say without their uniforms on.

And this is why I maintain a good relationship with law enforcement in the district, I thought while shaking my head in disbelief.

This was not any easy part of the job, but we were there for the safety of the students, staff, and community. I made the call to the police department and superintendent.

And so another Ave Ridge summer began.

CHAPTER 4

The Last Day of School!

June 17, 1964

I couldn't wait to get to school. It was the last day and the sooner I got there, the sooner it would be summer vacation. It was a dark, overcast, hot, and humid morning. I parked my bike in the fifth-grade section of the bike racks then lined up in the fifth-grade line for one last time. The bell rang and our teachers guided us into the building. The windows were wide-open to invite whatever relief a small breeze might offer.

My class sat quietly in the institutional-beige room that was stripped bare for the summer, designating another year in the books. The teacher tried to keep our interest with group word games, conversations, and—let's face it—whatever else it took.

The last day of school was also one of the very few days when there might be a sighting of Principal Rains, also referred to by senior staff as Claude. We knew Principal Rains existed. Our teachers would threaten to send us to his office if we weren't behaving and we would hear him occasionally on the morning announcements or get a brief glimpse of his silhouette against the closed shade of his office door. Once in a while, the sound of muddled conversation could be heard throughout the year from his office. Our parents mentioned his name from time to time when talking to friends. Other than that, he might as well have been invisible. We didn't even know what a principal did other than make us come to school.

Now prior to leaving for the summer, there was time for one parting shot by our teacher before our release at the bell. The distribution of small manila envelopes containing our final report cards with the hand-printed grades in blue ink. Our teacher seemed to take great delight handing them out individually to us, making direct eye contact with a poker face and what I assumed was a sincere "Have a wonderful summer!"

I opened the envelope. No red! That was a good sign. Of course, the most important part of this document was our middle school classroom assignments. It would take a good portion of the summer to try to piece together the intricate puzzle of who would be in our section next year in the new school. There was a blank space where our sixth-grade teacher's name would be, so we could only speculate which of the three teachers we would get.

Please don't let it be Ms. Obdurate, I thought.

"All right, class, line up! The dismissal bell is about to ring!" my teacher said. "Keep in line when we walk through the halls, be safe during the summer, and don't wait until August to do your summer reading assignments." (Parting shot number 2.)

The dismissal bell rang as we headed single file to the exit. I could see the light at the end of the tunnel. It was here. Finally!

The entire student body bolted to the bike racks while chanting, "No more pencils, no more books …" There were also other chants that if I were to introduce them at home, my summer vacation would have been spent locked up in my room.

My friends and I hopped on our Sting-Rays and left the school grounds as quickly as we could possibly pedal. Teachers were hugging each other. Some were talking to the parents of kids who got picked up at the end of each day. Others started their cars with looks on their faces like they had just been released from prison.

In my mind's eye, I could imagine, in about ten minutes, Principal Rains turning out all of the school lights and exiting the front door to lock up the building for the summer. He was free until September.

And so my fifth-grade summer began!

CHAPTER 5

And So Summer Begins

June 22

I entered the building with coffee and bagels for the summer crew. Summer hours were abbreviated, and attire was casual. But I did stress, "Don't look ridiculous."

I woke up my head custodian, Iggy, who was "resting his eyes" in the boiler room, and gave him a coffee and a wink. My next stop was my summer office staff made up of my executive administrative assistant, Mrs. Lass, director of guidance, Mrs. Keller, and her administrative assistant, Ms. Sharp, assistant principal, Mr. Minor, and our athletic director, Coach Slick.

Everyone enjoyed the coffee and bagels as they made small talk and got settled in for the summer. Several parents were already gathering at the guidance office entrance. Some insisted a mistake had been made when their little prodigies received their final grades from their teachers, and others tried to negotiate their children's need to attend summer school. Then there were the parents who wanted to send materials to an alternate college.

While their children were accepted to colleges and universities of a variety of academic notoriety, these parents chose the most prestigious. The university names would proudly be displayed next to their children's names in the senior banquet and graduation programs. The universities of choice were also displayed on their family's clothing, coffee cups, rear SUV windows, and so on. Once all the end-of-year festivities were done, it was time to reregister them at the county college.

Parents were also arriving to pay fines for students who had misplaced textbooks, supplies, laptops, and lanyards in an effort to retrieve their child's diploma or report cards. A few of our graduates (alumni) came back again. They just couldn't believe it was all over and took in the moment with tears in their eyes. We politely asked that they leave.

I reminded the staff of our first administrative team meeting at 10:00 a.m. in the conference room.

Afterward, I was looking forward to having lunch with my old childhood friend Tommy. He was currently serving as superintendent of schools in the next town over.

Mrs. Lass completed and sent out the agenda for our 10:00 a.m. meeting as follows:

Agenda

June 22

- Debrief Graduation Ceremony
- Vacancies & Hiring Committee
- Facility Summer Use
- Monthly Reports Due
- Informacion del Contacto
- Idiadikasis Programmatismou
- ZZZZZZZZZZZZZZZZZZZZZZZZZZZZZZZZZZ

Please Initial

_____ Dr. Strat, Principal

_____ Mr. Minor, Assistant Principal

_____ Coach Slick, Athletic Director
_____ Mrs. Lass, Executive Administrative Assistant
_____ Mrs. Keller, Director of Guidance
_____ Ms. Sharp, Guidance Administrative Assistant

As ten o'clock arrived, so did the summer team. Coffee was ready as we comfortably sat around the conference table telling a few jokes and taking verbal shots at each other. I called the meeting to order and began with a review of the senior graduation ceremony. Laughter, head shaking, and eye-rolling led into comments the equivalent of "Well, there's always next year."

The meeting continued with my abbreviated staff bandying about the most current educational buzzwords. I myself liked to stick with the standards. For example, every time someone used any form of the word *collaborate,* I took an extra sip of my coffee. The extra caffeine not only kept the meeting moving with a bit more alacrity but had also proven to keep me quite regular throughout the years. I've found it to be a good practice to have coffee at the ready during any administrative meetings. If there could be food or snacks, it would be even better.

I began to distribute copies of the applications we received so far for the staff vacancies. We reviewed them together, rated them according to the district's rubric *(buzzword?),* and blocked out dates for interviews. We discussed combining responsibilities for members of our team who had been released as of June 30. These positions were integral to the success of our overall programs. However, in the board's infinite wisdom, if they didn't understand what the position was, they reasoned, "Why not just save on the budget?" This included instructional supervisor, in-class support, director of DEI, child study team, and the ABE program. *(A Basic Education?)*

I shared with my team the benefits of doing initial interviews by phone. This could save each of us an enormous amount of time.

This, combined with running background checks on social media (OMG) could get you to the elimination rounds quicker than anticipated. I also reminded the team that as active administrators, they should block and/or completely proofread and edit any social media they may be on.

"Holding a red plastic cup in your selfies is not your friend!" I reinforced.

I could see the group's interest waning by the way they pretended to be taking copious notes while in fact checking their emails. Since the majority of attendees present at this morning's meeting were wearing glasses, it was not difficult to view their laptop screens reflecting off of their Armani's and Dolce Cabanas. Others had successfully won two out of three games of solitaire on their personal tablets.

Finally I emphasized, "We will meet again on Thursday to confirm our summer calendared events!"

As the meeting closed, Mrs. Lass informed me she would be going to her doctor's office during her lunch break. Apparently while leaving the graduation ceremony last evening, she tripped over a board member sleeping off his liquid dinner on the ten-yard line. Yes, yes ... There were photos already circulating on all social media sites and then some. And yes, the board member was proudly sharing the pictures with the traditional smiley emoji and a thumbs up. Campaign season started early this year.

Mrs. Lass was my rock. Her historical knowledge of the district was legendary. She never got rattled, was always positive and smiling, and above all, had my back. Let's face it: she ran the show, and without her, I would be lost.

Midday rolled around and it was now time for me to take an extended lunch to catch up with my childhood friend Tommy. Our usual meeting place was Jazzy's Diner, an out-of-town establishment off the beaten trail. Gotta love summer hours ...

There was less traffic today due to the area schools being out for the summer. I pulled into the diner lot and parked in the back, hoping my car would not be recognized. Jazzy's was filling up for the lunch rush.

As I made my way through the foyer, I saw Tommy waving me over to a booth in the back, out of earshot range to potential eavesdroppers. When it came to confidentiality, whether in district or out of district, you knew you'd be held responsible for discussing students, staff, or personnel. If you could hear the others where you were, they could hear you!

Tommy and I sat down and congratulated each other on the completion of another school year. "One year closer to retirement!" I said as our waitress stopped by to take our order and bring us our first cups of coffee.

Midway through our conversation, our attention was drawn to a table across the room. Two men and one woman in their early twenties were loudly discussing their adventures as substitute teachers in both Tommy's and my school districts. They obviously didn't know we were here as they mentioned full names of teachers and students they wouldn't mind dating or—well, let's just keep it at dating. This is called the "Would ya'?" game." Others involved a ten-foot pole. They then all agreed, "Substituting is easy money for sitting in a classroom doin' nuthin'! Teachers have it easy!" Their voices dropped as they continued to brag about their personal weekend conquests, ability to maintain large amounts of contraband substances, etc.

Ahh, confidentiality at its finest!

I was going to have to address this breach of confidentiality when I arrived back to the office. Teachers and administrators were held at a higher level of accountability. Tommy and I looked at each other, shook our heads, and thought how even a harmless lunch could have ramifications. This was definitely not just a nine-to-five job.

Our conversation drifted to the great times we had had during summer vacations when we were just kids in the neighborhood. It brought back so many fantastic memories. We paused, raised our coffee cups, and toasted the old days.

Two protein omelets, and six cups of coffee between us later, it was time to get back to our buildings. The last thing I said before leaving was "I want another fifth-grade summer!" Life was so much simpler back then.

Tommy nodded and said, "If only ..."

Following an enjoyable and lengthy lunch, I returned to my building only to be greeted in the main office by several resolute PTO mothers accompanied by Mrs. Keller, the director of guidance. Mrs. Keller explained to me that for the past four weeks, the PTO had taken it upon themselves to form a special committee to assist us with the scheduling of their children for the next school year.

These thoughtful parents had offered not one, not two, but three alternate schedules customized to address the needs of their individual offspring. These documents, including graphs and spreadsheets, were very detailed. They included their recommendations for teachers for their children, the most convenient parking spots, who should be in the same lunch period together, and where their lockers should be located. The study hall for all involved should be first period. This was a must since seniors needed more rest than, dare I say, underclassmen.

I thought, *Brilliant! After all the schooling, studying, on-the-job experiences, and endless hours laboring over the master schedule each and every year, I never once thought how much time and effort I could have saved myself if I just let the parents and students develop their own schedules!*

An hour and fifteen minutes later, the placating session was over. We smiled, laughed, and wished each other a wonderful summer. As I closed my office door, there was a moment of complete silence, including a deep breath and blank locked stares between Mrs. Keller and me. Not a word was said. Just an understanding nod as she left my office.

I asked Mrs. Lass to come in so we could begin the monumental task of sorting out the summer in an effort to be ready for the first day of school in September. Mrs. Lass came in on crutches, sat down, looked at me, and gave a clenched smile.

I said, "Ooooooohhhh, what's up?"

She explained that the nasty spill she had taken over the napping board member at our graduation ceremony had left her with a cracked hip and spiral fracture. She would need to take most of the summer off on medical leave for surgery and to recover.

I was concerned for her health and understood the situation. She said her son was waiting outside to load up some of her belongings and to drive her home.

I helped her gather up her things and walked close by her side to the parking lot. I was worried about her, but I would be lying if I said my mind wasn't racing about how much more difficult my next few months would become.

Her son was waiting in his jacked-up super truck. He came around, opened the door, picked her up like a toddler, sat her in the seat, buckled her in, and then zoomed off.

I stood motionless in the parking lot, like you would see in any B movie, staring at the truck as it got smaller and smaller in the distance.

I thought, *I'll just meet with my other office staff members tomorrow morning to explain the situation and distribute Mrs. Lass's workload for the summer.*

Oh wait. Together they couldn't unjam the copier!

"I am soooo &@%#!"

CHAPTER 6

First Day of Freedom!

June 18, 1964

My neighborhood was a great place to be in the summertime. Although the street I lived on was straight and level containing approximately forty houses, there were two distinct neighborhoods. The lower numbers were kids my age, and upper numbers were the older kids who were a good two or three years older than we were. The entire block connected to main roads on either end, making our road one of many rungs in a ladder if viewed from above.

The neighbors all got along well watching each other's kids and yards day and night. But every neighborhood seemed to have that one house. You know the one where that elderly couple lived. One was a grumpy old soul. The kind who would yell, "You damn kids ... Stay off my lawn!" if he had the chance. I'm sure he could easily outrun any of us if a ball or Frisbee accidentally landed anywhere on his property. And though I'm not completely sure, I think he had a trusty ol' rock salt gun by his side whenever we had a pickup kickball game in the road. His partner, on the other hand, was pleasant enough and waved and smiled at us when we were around. He was a good ten years older than the grumpy one, but it looked the other way around.

My house was centrally located on our half of the block. So after shoveling down a bowl of Wheaties and milk, covered by an equal amount of sugar, I hopped on my Sting-Ray bike and rode to the end of my driveway. Over the next few minutes, the gang, all on bikes, would gravitate toward the driveway like magnets.

Peter lived next door, to the right, in the white colonial house. He had two brothers who were younger by several years. We didn't see them much since they mostly choose to play alone in their backyard.

Micky lived next door to Peter in a green Cape Cod. His only brother was years older and over in Vietnam. He didn't hear from him much, but you could tell he missed him.

Keith lived two houses down in the other direction in a raised Cape. He didn't have any brothers or sisters so he spent a lot of time outside waiting to see when his friends would come out.

Roger was my best friend. He lived across the street in a house similar to mine. He had two younger sisters, Jill and Carol. They were twins and slightly annoying.

For the rest of the morning, we rode our bikes up and down our half of the block aimlessly, shaking off the residue of another school year. Eventually, we rode single file to the corner store located conveniently on the corner of the block. After all, it was lunchtime, and nothing said "lunch" better than Twinkies, Yankee Doodles, and Bazooka Bubblegum. We entered the store and were greeted by the familiar faces behind the counters. After making our selections, we met back out in the front parking lot and sat on old milk crates leaning against the side of the building. It felt like summer already.

Afterward, having had our nourishment for the time being, we headed to the ball field, which was located two blocks over, to see if we could get a pickup baseball game going. Thus, the Bazooka!

There were kids our age hanging around field three, the lesser choice of the four fields available, so we parked our bikes and brought our mitts and bats to the dugout. We counted up those of us playing and chose up sides, which was about five to a team. We rotated positions each inning, but when Tommy was there, he was always the pitcher. That we all agreed on.

Tommy was missing today. During the year, he would arrive at school each day on the little yellow bus and all his classes were in the small classroom at the end of the hallway. He was a great kid, and during the summer, he was the first one chosen for a pickup baseball game. He was an awesome player. Although he was not here today, you could bet he'd be here all summer long.

This was the perfect afternoon for a game. Sunny and breezy with a comfortable temperature.

During the first two innings, the red tinting on our arms, legs, and any other exposed body parts was getting just a little deeper.

As we started the third inning, my closest friend Roger got hit by a wild pitch. An all-out brawl ensued involving pushing, fists, the throwing of equipment and dirt, explicit kid language, and a flying bat. A few short moments later, we stopped, looked at each other, brushed off, began to laugh, then picked up the game where we left off. This was what summer was all about. Independence, hangin' with your buddies, letting off steam, growing, and learning how to get along. I was sure this was the way it would be for generations to come.

Numerous girls from our school slowly gathered on the portable bleachers. We peacocked up to show them how guys have fun, occasionally glancing over to see if they were still watching. They were chattering and giggling throughout the entire inning of play. This was a little distracting, so when the inning ended, Peter shouted jokingly, "Hey! If you wanna get your sneakers dirty, we'll do an inning of boys against girls!"

They said yes … We looked at each other, then in unison shot a not so enthusiastic glance in Peter's direction. Peter shrugged and smiled like it was no big deal.

The girls huddled up to get organized. Keith's twin sisters, Jill and Carol, were the first two batters in the lineup. Peter was pitching and searching for a way to redeem himself.

He announced, "No underhand pitching here. *Real baseball!*"

The girls looked at each other, smiled, and shrugged their shoulders.

Peter threw the first pitch, almost skimming Jill's elbow. Great strategy to "shake 'em up." Jill squinted with a stone-cold face and stepped back into the batter's box. Smirks and chuckles were heard throughout the infield. The next pitch was a swing and a miss. More of the same from the infield. With a showy windup, he lobbed the next ball toward Jill. She got a good piece of it, and it grounded through the infield, having Micky race to try to scoop it up in center. He fumbled a bit as Jill landed on second base. There was a visible attitude adjustment on the side of the boys. Peter played this off as just warming up.

Looking toward second base, he muttered with a droll look on his face, "Lucky hit."

"Now we're gonna get serious. Right, guys?" Peter exclaimed as Carol stepped up to the plate.

Loud whispers of "Whiffer" and "Belly itcher" could be heard from around the field, accompanied by random swaying back and forth by the boys so as to not have a repeat of the previous batter. The first pitch was straight over the plate as a crack of the bat could be heard by neighbors for several blocks. Over the outfielders it went, and the score was now 2–zip, no outs. The girls' team was jumping up and down and screaming as the two hitters crossed home plate. We stood motionless and expressionless for what seemed like an eternity then went back to our positions, trying not to make eye contact with anyone on their team.

Next in the lineup was Ellen, a petite, shy, little girl who lived a few blocks from the field. She was the youngest of thirteen brothers and sisters. Although she was quiet, she was popular in our class. Our parents were close friends so we saw each other throughout the year outside of school.

Peter was back to his original state of humiliation. Without making eye contact, he said to Ellen in a low, broken voice, "Ready?"

Ellen smiled, giggled, and replied, "I guess so," as she shrugged.

The first two pitches were way outside, trying to get her to swing.

A voice from the field shouted, "The breeze from the ball is going to blow her over!"

A burst of laughter erupted. Even a teammate or two of hers showed a slight grin.

Ellen stepped back into the batter's box, looking into the field with a smile suggesting which of her fingers she would like us to notice. Another pitch straight down the middle and Ellen connected like a pro. Right over the centerfielder. She giggled and jumped up and down screaming, *"Do I run?"*

Her teammates all shouted, "Run!"

She began to run, stopping at each base while waiting for her friends to guide her back home. With a beaming grin, Ellen crossed home plate. I can't be sure, but I believe I saw Peter slightly hunched over and wiping away a tear as he cleared his throat.

At this point, we suggested it would be in the best interest of all involved that we should probably stop the game. Ya' know … for water … rest … ya' know …

The girls stared us down with their hands on their hips and said, *"Really?"* Their facial expressions said a lot more.

We, of course, justified this in the usual way by making up any excuse that seemed semireasonable to get out of this predicament.

Keith said, in his own smooth and articulate manner, "Yeah,

we have stuff to do. Ya' know ... stuff and things not here that we ... Important ... stuff ... now!"

The girls stared in awe of his brilliance, shook their heads, then turned to walk off the field.

"I wish Tommy was here," I whispered to Roger.

For the remainder of the summer, the events of this game would not be spoken about. Especially to Tommy.

CHAPTER 7

It Can't Get Any Worse

June 23

The silence of the building first thing in the morning was interrupted with my announcement over the PA system.

"All hands on deck! All hands on deck! Mrs. Lass is out for the summer. This is not a drill! I repeat. Mrs. Lass is out for the summer. Report to the conference room, stat!"

It was 8:30 a.m. sharp as the staff arrived, skidding into the room. Some looked pale, others confused. My assistant principal, Mr. Minor, was hyperventilating into his lunch bag! *Get the lifeboats ready. It's gonna be a rough ride!*

I took my place at the helm of the large, rectangular table, adjusting my custom-made chair that had a striking resemblance to the captain's chair on the original *USS Enterprise*. My crew— rather, staff—was preparing themselves for the storm. Even worse, there was no coffee!

"I don't need to tell you what we're in for. Some of you may actually have to work this summer. I've prepared a comprehensive PowerPoint presentation detailing what we, as a collective group, know and what we don't," I began.

Several gasps and whimpers were faintly heard as I continued.

Slide 1 said, "Where does Mrs. Lass keep everything? Anyone?" I glanced around the room. My assistant principal was typing away. I believe he was updating his resume. This meeting was going to last forever.

Slide 2 said, "Who knows how to use the coffee maker? Anyone?"

Again, blank stares with mouths gaped open.

"No one?" Things were looking pretty grim.

As I was changing to slide 3, an email popped up on the screen that was visible for all to see. It was from Mrs. Lass.

Should I open it in front of the team? I thought. *Why not? What do I have to lose?*

My shaking hand slowly opened the email. A wince, a glance, and then a moment of contemplation. This was followed by an outburst of cheers, laughter, and sighs of relief. My assistant principal made the sign of the cross then pointed to the heavens. Mrs. Lass had spent the entire night detailing day-by-day, week-by-week instructions, with diagrams, of what needed to be done and where everything was located. Calamity averted! I kept a calm outward appearance, but deep down my stomach sank into the boiler room. I realized we might actually get through this.

My assistant principal took notes as I assigned duties to the team. They were all receptive, smiling, and nodding in agreement. But I wasn't fooled. I knew exactly what they were thinking. And it wasn't pretty.

In anticipation of a difficult day, I extended our lunchtime and had the local deli, the Hefty King, deliver their best. On me, of course. Throughout this time, mild conversation took place, but most of the team's faces were glued to the screens of their cell phones and laptops. Oddly enough, I believe they were texting and emailing each other. So much easier than looking each other in the eye and having an actual conversation. It wasn't so long ago I was in their shoes. I would be doing the same thing.

Following our lunch "social," we headed back to the main office.

The afternoon began with a bang. Mrs. Sycoe, the parent of Sidney Sycoe, a soon-to-be sophomore in my educational establishment, slammed my office door open and began her maniacal rant. Sidney was no stranger to either Mr. Minor's or Mrs. Keller's offices. Unfortunately, Mrs. Lass was not here to run interference for me.

"Dr. Strat!" she shouted. "This school continues to let my son down and nothing ever gets done!" In an even louder voice, she shouted, "*What are you going to do about it?* I'm calling my lawyer. The board will get a piece of my mind at the next public meeting, and I'm bringing reporters! He's not going to waste his time in summer school for failing gym. That's not even a class!"

In a calm low tone, I said, "Coffee?"

In the same low tone, she replied, "Yes, please."

She continued her rant. "I've had it up to here with your teachers and administrators constantly picking on Sidney for no reason at all! And now he has to go to summer school? Not going to happen! You'll be out of a job first! I'll own your house!"

In my same low, calm voice, I asked, "Cream? Sugar?"

She replied again in a low, calm voice, "Just a little cream. Thank you!"

The histrionics went on for another good five minutes. She was really on a roll today, and with new material, too!

She finally let out an audible sigh then sat down as I handed her the coffee.

"You good?" I asked.

"Yeah, I'm good," she said as she took a sip. Beginning to tear up, she said, "What am I going to do, Dr. Strat? He's driving me crazy!"

Already there! I thought.

We continued with our usual cordial meeting talking about

everything from the weather to the New York Yankees' chances of winning the pennant this year. Mrs. Sycoe's venting session was coming to an end. She did understand summer school was required for Sydney to move up to the next grade. Actually, she understood this before she came into my office. Sometimes I believed my degree should read "principal/therapist."

The meeting wrapped up with her thanking me for the coffee and wishing me a good day. This, I thought, was never part of my university training.

The remainder of the afternoon was uneventful, until at the end of the day, Mr. Minor, my assistant principal of two years, entered my office, twitching and stammering, to inform me he was putting in his sixty-day notice. He was taking a position as an actuary where he could pursue a career that was less stressful. This was a decision he had been discussing with his psychologist, neurologist, and pharmacist. He also requested to be released sooner if at all possible. I can't say I didn't see this coming. His first year and a half out of the classroom and as a new administrator was impressive. He seemed to lose a bit of steam since January but was still eager to perform his duties. Once he signed his new contract in May for the upcoming year, he confided in me he was under a lot of stress at home and on the job. The medication and therapy disclosure came right after graduation.

I offered him a seat and a cup of coffee to discuss his decision. There he just sat, staring off into the wilderness of his mind. Twitching a little, then stammering, "Th-thank you for un-understanding, Doc."

He left my office moments later relieved and still stressed at the same time. I watched him bump into the counter twice as he made his way back to his office.

Prior to leaving for the day, I posted all vacancies on local and social media. The vacancy for assistant principal was in larger and bolder font.

Meanwhile, we did receive four applications for our AP physics opening. One was written in crayon. Since it was a nightmare trying to fill the vacancy, we set up interviews for all four.

Could this summer get any better? I thought.

CHAPTER 8

TJ, Dexie, Joey, and Bud

Summer 1964

I have a close family, but even close families don't hang out together all the time. After all, it was summertime and we had our neighborhood cliques and subcliques.

My brother TJ was three years ahead of me in school so he would be a freshman this year. He was the strong and adventurous type, super intense, and wouldn't let anyone get in his way if he had a goal in mind. He was involved in several sports like soccer and track, loved to do martial arts, and worked out with weights whenever he could. TJ also read a lot and liked to draw. He was a good brother, as far as brothers went, but if he got mad at you, watch out. Once he was mad at my younger brother Bud, and he picked me up and threw me at him.

TJ liked working with tools and couldn't wait to get his driver's license. His prize possession was his black Schwinn Sting-Ray bike with chopper handlebars and a tiger banana seat because he built it himself. He and his friends had a ritual of rummaging through the town junkyard then dragging home bicycle parts. They got together in our backyard carefully piecing together and improving their prize rides throughout the summer months. Once a year our town had junk day when everyone could discard all their large junk and broken equipment they had been eager to get rid of. TJ called this day the annual junk buffet.

This year, he was customizing his prize possession by cutting the front forks off an old bike frame then bolting them on to the existing front forks on his Schwinn. This would give the bike a mean chopper appearance and make it easier to do wheelies! My dad tried to be supportive but was more of an academic and a bit of a neat freak. An office guy. Seeing a miniature junkyard expanding in our backyard drove him crazy. He would cut the lawn around the junk each week in Haggar navy blue slacks, black dress shoes, and an older white dress shirt. I knew he would've liked to help TJ with his hobbies, but I don't think he knew how.

My sister Dexie was two years ahead of me in school and got good grades, especially in math and science, which I really don't get because no one likes math and science. She's weird. Her favorite class was gym, and she was good at it too. She was always full of energy and could be seen running, biking, climbing trees, and doing cartwheels nonstop. I'm not sure she ever slept.

My youngest brother Bud was two years younger than me. When I wasn't hanging out with my friends, he and I would team up. Bud helped Mom garden and work in the yard because he liked plants and loved the outdoors. I'm sure if he could live back in the woods, he would. He was kinda quiet but made friends wherever he went.

I myself was a combination of my siblings. I did all right in school. When I played sports, I preferred neighborhood pickup games to town league stuff. Teachers picked me as the lead in most class plays because I was pretty good at music and memorizing stuff. Plus I didn't mind a good crowd. My mother said I was a ham. She even sent me to local acting classes and theater groups. I loved to read books. Any kind of books. I even had a special bookcase in my bedroom where I proudly displayed them once I was done reading them. I also liked to sit at the upright piano in the back room trying to pick out songs and pretend I was on tour in a rock and roll band. But most of all, I wanted to play guitar.

I did get a plastic guitar with nylon strings for Christmas the past year. I wasn't crazy about how it sounded so that week I biked over to the music store on the other side of town and bought steel strings, convinced they would make it sound more electric. I couldn't wait to put them on and crank out some Elvis.

I raced home to begin my rock and roll career! I remember the excitement growing as I tightened the six steel beauties. Tighter, tighter, tighter, then ... Then there were two. Two pieces of plastic guitar held together with steel cables dangling off my lap. I was on the verge of tears.

"What have I done?" I cried.

My siblings, of course, were laughing so hard they couldn't breathe. TJ was coughing and turning so red with laughter I thought he was gonna puke. I remember storming out of the room with my guitar carcass in tow. I went up to my bedroom and slammed the door shut then sat on the bed looking at what used to be my guitar. Now it was just a pile of chipped plastic.

After a little time went by and I gathered what was left of my dignity, I thought, *Yeah, OK, that was pretty funny* ... But I would never let them know that ... Wouldn't give them the satisfaction.

That summer I was going to build my own guitar. I had a two-by-four and some plywood out in the shed. The steel strings were still in great shape. How hard could it be?

CHAPTER 9

Time to Take a Break

June 24

It was a tough week so checking the time, we concluded that Friday night rush hour was just about lightening up. Impulsively, we decided to drive down to our shore house for the weekend. It was only an hour and a half away. As a kid, going on the beach, even for a few hours, seemed like an eternity.

When we arrived, my wife went right to sleep. I, on the other hand, went out to my back porch to smell the ocean air. The only thing that relaxed me more was watching the waves come in and sitting on the back porch playing my acoustic guitar. The temperature was in the low seventies with a mild breeze and clear sky.

I closed my eyes and began playing some old classic rock ballads while thinking about the summer months ahead. I smiled as my mind drifted to the ocean, waves, salt air, sand, scheduling, curriculum, interviews … I snapped open my eyes and stopped playing. It was Sunday evening! Time to drive back home.

"It's going to be that kind of summer," I said to myself.

CHAPTER 10

Down the Shore

June 20, 1964

The weekend was here, and my parents were taking us down the shore. (Yes, I'm from New Jersey.) We sat around the dining table in our bathing suits and sandals as Mom brought out a special breakfast of Taylor ham, egg, and cheese on a hard roll. (Yes, I'm from North Jersey.) We ate fast so we could get on the road and beat the traffic.

Dad packed up the ol' 1957 Ford Ranch Station Wagon with all the equipment anyone could possibly need for a day at the beach. My older brother and sister rode in the back seat while my younger brother Bud and I took our usual place in the way back of the wagon. Dad strategically placed towels, coolers, and chairs to cover the two-foot, rotted holes on the floor over each wheel well.

Once on the road, Bud and I sat with our arms hanging out the back flip up window waving and making faces at the cars behind us for most of the trip. The highlight was playing punch buggy when we saw a red Volkswagen Beetle drive by. The last time we went to the shore, we counted thirty-eight Buggies on the ride down. Boy can my brother punch!

There were a lot more cars on the road as we got closer to the shore, but Dad still managed to find a parking spot close to the beach entrance. He could always sense when there was a closer spot. He parked cutting off two other cars, then we all helped unload the wagon and dragged everything to a spot close to the water.

Dad spent a good part of our first hour on the beach trying to inflate four canvas rafts. Blue on one side, yellow on the other for my brothers and me; blue on one side, red on the other for Dexie.

While Dad was busy with the rafts, we ran into the ocean hip deep at first, then dove into the waves one by one. The taste of saltwater was refreshing. There weren't a lot of people around this early in the morning so we had most of the ocean to ourselves.

A short time later, I saw my dad collapse in the sand after inflating the final raft. It was time! We ran up and grabbed our rafts then ran back into the water as my mother finished setting up the blankets, chairs, coolers … well, everything, while Dad remained exhausted, face down in the sand, gasping for air.

Mom shouted, "Be careful, kids!" then proceeded to slather olive oil all over her body.

The waves were just right. Not too rough, not too calm. Perfect for rafting. We waited, all lined up next to each other for the perfect wave to push us back to the beach. This took some time, but it was definitely worth it once it happened. More kids joined in as the morning went on and the beach got more crowded.

As we approached late morning, dead jellyfish engulfed us. This was the perfect opportunity to use them as water balloons. We were in our glory. Well, except for Bud, who was the prime target.

"Must be fun being the youngest!" I shouted while Bud kept ducking the steady stream of flying jellyfish.

The lifeguard made several attempts to stop all of us from flinging jellyfish around. This was a useless attempt. Eventually he gave up and went back to twirling the long red string of his whistle around his finger.

About an hour later, our mom called to us, "Lunch, kids! Come on ... Now!"

We dragged our way to the beach blanket and feasted on PB&J's and baloney and cheese sandwiches. Grape Kool-Aid was passed out by Mom in our Flintstone glasses collected from our many visits to the Esso station. Dad lifted his face from the sand and joined us. Mom laughed at how red our shoulders and backs were getting. She, on the other hand, was taking on a shade that resembled the red punch buggies we counted on the way down.

A few blankets down, I noticed a yellow polka dot bikini. There was something familiar about the wearer of the bikini, but I just couldn't place it. It would come to me, but I knew it was going to bother me the rest of the day.

Following the obligatory wait of a half hour before going back in the water, the festivities resumed. Mom and Dad finally came waist deep into the water, splashed themselves, then went back to baking in the sun. Dad fell asleep on the sand for most of the afternoon. We, on the other hand, never left the water. The waves were just right!

Bud walked toward a random group of kids his age who had shovels and pails making sandcastles at the shoreline. He sat with them and began digging while introducing himself. Within five seconds, he was part of the family. This was his superpower. He could blend in anywhere.

TJ, Dexie, and I stood knee deep in the waves just watching people. Most girls Dexie's age were sunning themselves in groups on their towels. Boys TJ's age walked by alone or in small groups waving and saying, "Hi!" to us. Well, it was mostly directed at Dexie.

We were back in the water without our rafts. It was bodysurfing time. This took a little more skill than depending on your raft to keep you afloat, but you also wound up with a lot more sand in your bathing suit.

We continued bodysurfing even though our shoulders and backs were taking on a darker shade of red, but we didn't feel a thing. Mom and Dad, on the other hand, were asleep on the blanket still a few shades of red darker than us.

As the afternoon went on, the tide came in slowly and was almost at the blanket. Dexie ran up and nudged Mom just in time. Dad? Well, Dad was woken up with the next wave. I guess what's funny to one person may not be funny to another. Especially if you're shocked awake with cold water.

After a few choice words and gestures by Dad, and several other dads across the beach, we all helped drag the wet blanket and towels up to higher ground. Even Bud stepped away from his responsibilities as foreman of the sandcastle construction team to lend a helping hand.

While our stuff dried out, Mom and Dad walked us to the boardwalk. Our beach was at the beginning—or end of the boardwalk, depending on how you looked at it.

We were already pretty tired as we started walking the boards. You would think we would be more enthusiastic about going on the rides and playing games. I guess we were getting older, and the rides were more for the younger kids. The higher and faster rides had long lines, and we'd been on them before.

Either way, we walked by games of chance, burger and pizza stands, and some rides and decided instead on ice cream at Mister Softee! This was the best ice cream you could get. I got the chocolate and vanilla swirl cone that I knew from experience I had to eat fast, or it would melt down my arm like … well, like Bud. I guess that's why Mom always grabbed a handful of napkins wherever we went. We ate our ice cream and stared at the ocean for a while then headed back down the boards.

Dad gave us change to play a few pinball machines in the

arcade before we headed back to the beach to pack up. We usually fought to stay on the boardwalk and go on rides, but we were all pretty tired, and the first signs of pain that only sunburn could realize was starting to make an appearance.

Older kids were now getting onto the boardwalk in groups. The girls waved at TJ, maybe because he was wearing a sleeveless shirt. I mean he had been working out. The boys were waving at Dexie. I didn't know why, but she waved back in a shy way that was really not like Dexie at all.

Mom and Dad also looked like they were getting tired. Everyone agreed it was a fun but exhausting day.

My brothers, sister, and I helped gather up all the blankets and towels while Dad pulled up the car as close as he could get to the beach. We loaded up the car in record time then headed back home with the windows wide-open to get as much breeze going through the car as possible.

After punch buggy eighteen, it came to me.

"Ms. Obdurate!" I shouted in a high-pitched voice that I'm certain woke up many a dog in the area. That was who was wearing the yellow polka dot bikini.

I suddenly felt the bologna and cheese sandwich, Kool-Aid, and ice cream working their way up from the depths of my stomach, as I remembered the image. How could I ever look at her the same way again? If I got her as my sixth-grade teacher, I'd …

That was when the daily contents of my stomach made an encore appearance that I'm certain didn't please the car behind us. Mom and Dad glanced back, looked at each other, then continued the long ride home. The traffic was building up and the car grew hotter every time we slowed down. It was like being in an oven. This did not help my stomach or my shoulders.

We finally pulled into the driveway, helped unload the car, then dragged ourselves to our bedrooms. The sharp sunburn numbness and pain shooting from our shoulders and backs continued making their debuts.

I checked the freezer for comfort. There were no ice cubes left in the metal trays because Mom and Dad already split them up, wrapped them in towels, and were spreading them across their scorched bodies. I would take a really cold shower, but TJ and Bud were already banging on the door of the one bathroom we had for Dexie to hurry up and get out. The odds were against them. I wouldn't wish this pain on anyone, but it didn't stop me from smacking Bud on the back as I walked by.

I turned on my old floor fan and tried my best to fall asleep in front of it.

"Oh the pain!" I groaned a half hour later.

From each bedroom, I could hear the same.

For the remainder of the weekend, we huddled as close to our fans as we could possibly get. Dad left the house only once to get a vat of Noxzema to share with our family of burn victims.

CHAPTER 11

Interviews

June 28

It was Wednesday morning, the last week of June. Saturday would be the Fourth of July. A four-day weekend!

Mr. Minor, Coach Slick, and my supervisor of building and grounds, Iggy, began our 9:00 a.m. meeting to discuss this summer's Battle of the Fields.

Coach Slick began by laying out a network of hand-drawn maps, charts, and graphs with scribbles and arrows pointing out ... I don't now ... the war zone? He continued by delineating times, rotations, spectator expectations, bus and restroom usage, helipads, network coverage. The usual.

As he finished his presentation, he asked, "Are there any questions?"

Dead silence.

"*What?* I spent weeks on this!" Coach said, sounding a little deflated.

Here we go, I thought. Coach was a relatively mild-mannered guy, until you uncovered a weakness in his scheduling abilities. Then Dr. Banner either maintained his dignity or the Hulk took over. Usually the latter.

In rapid succession, the comments began.

Iggy started with a deadpan face. "I don't have enough men for this."

Mr. Minor was next. "You forgot the marching band and cheerleaders."

While stirring my coffee, I said, "The budget won't cover all the buses. We're down two drivers."

Iggy jumped in again. "The football field has just been seeded and can't be used for two weeks."

With a growing smirk on his face, Mr. Minor continued. "They found traces of radon on the soccer field. They're ripping it out after the Fourth of July."

To give Coach a chance to gain his composure, I offered, "Coffee anyone?"

Mr. Minor jumped right back in. "The neighbors are complaining that practices start too early. The noise is waking up their preschoolers."

Iggy continued the list in a lower, calmer voice. "The gymnasium floor is being refinished early this school year due to scheduling issues. Probably the second week of July."

Trying once again to offer a break in the rapid fire, I offered, "Bagel, anyone?"

Iggy went right on looking Coach directly in the eyes, "The girls' locker room will be closed for two weeks. A cherry bomb exploded in one of the toilets graduation night. I think the board president did it."

Seeing the green monster growing in size right in front of me, I said with a smile, "Plan B, Coach?"

Coach Slick threw his keys against the wall.

"$&@#!" he shouted. His following remarks were even worse.

The meeting deteriorated with Coach pounding the table with his fists (almost knocking my coffee over), ripping up papers, windshield-wiping their remains to the floor, then storming out of the room.

That went well, I thought.

We ended the meeting knowing that after a cooling down period, Coach would regroup and try again. That was classic Coach.

Maybe the interviews this afternoon would go better. We would be interviewing our four candidates for the AP physics vacancy.

The morning dragged on, but I did manage a ten-minute break for a PB&J and coffee. I then headed to the conference room, where the others arrived almost immediately after so we could get acclimated for the unexpected that an interview process could realize.

Following a review of the candidates' resumes, our 12:30 p.m. candidate was brought in the room by Ms. Frenzy, who was filling in for Mrs. Lass during her medical leave. She was already shaking her head left to right with her eyes mostly closed as she introduced Ms. Pert.

Ms. Pert was a recent graduate from one of our more prestigious state universities. She entered the room wearing cutoff jeans, a tank top, and sandals and chewing at least four sticks of spearmint gum. She apologized for being a little "out of it" as she went on to detail the great party she just couldn't leave last evening. And yes, she was the one who submitted her resume in crayon.

Dr. Rod, our 1:15 p.m. interview, was candidate number 2. He moved two hours north to our area after teaching for twelve years in his previous district. He was middle-aged and wore his long, straight, silver hair in a manbun.

Mrs. Stout, our 2:00 p.m. interview, was candidate number 3. She was a younger yet experienced woman in her early thirties. The business suit she was wearing was in school colors.

Mr. Johnson, our 2:45 p.m. interview, was candidate number

4 who moved here from Chicago and was eager to continue his nine-year career in our area.

I opened with the first question. "Let's start out by getting to know a little bit about you. Could you tell us something about yourself that isn't on your resume?"

Candidate 1 said, "I really like science and would love to land a teaching job so I can spend my summers at the shore."

Candidate 2, while staring directly at the floor, said, "Well, I have a podcast for teenagers to help them understand physics. I would spend all my time with teenagers if I could."

Candidate 3 said, "I'm an avid reader. I play guitar and sing in my church choir." She smiled brightly and made eye contact with all of us as she spoke. "I have a wonderful husband, who is also a high school science teacher, and I'm blessed with two teenage daughters."

Candidate 4 said, "I'm the product of the United States Air Force. I coach several sports for our local Boys & Girls Club to give back to the community. I love pizza and have a golden retriever named Major."

Mr. Minor asked the second question. "What do you know about our Ave Ridge High School and community?"

Candidate 1 said, "I really didn't have much time to check out your web site. You do have a web site, right?"

Candidate 2 said, "I'm just learning about the area, but after looking over your web site, I see you have a lot of freshmen boys' sports."

Candidate 3 said, "I drove through the community over the weekend. It seems like a lovely town. I read through the school web site and was very impressed by the amount of sports and activities you offer. *The Student/Parent Handbook* is a wonderful resource for parents and students. I also read through the course offerings and curriculum outlines. I can't wait to dig in deeper."

Candidate 4 said, "Small town, mixed demographics, powder blue collar community, visible police presence."

Mrs. Keller asked question 3. "How do you earn your students' trust?"

Candidate 1 said, "I get along with everyone. And if they like science, they will trust me ... Trust me!" She giggled.

Candidate 2 said, "When I walk around the lab tables, I compliment the students, pat them on the back, and say, 'Good job!' The boys usually appreciate this a lot."

Candidate 3 said, "I believe trust is a two-way street and has to be earned. We discuss and understand the expectations and desired outcomes of the class and respect each other's opinions. Every student is different and should be instructed at their own pace, even in AP coursework."

Candidate 4 said, "Within the first week, they fall into place. I don't accept anything less. If they're in an AP course, they do the work or get out."

I asked question 4. "Why do you want to work here?"

Candidate 1 said, "I guess it's a good place to start my career."

Candidate 2 said, "I can't seem to get a job since Megan's Law."

"Thank you for coming in, Dr. Rod," I said. "Let me show you out."

Candidate 3 said, "The district I'm currently with has eliminated their AP courses and most of their honors courses. I love the kids and staff, but I don't see much of a future there since I was the last one hired in the department."

Candidate 4 said, "Need a job. I'm willing to roll up my sleeves and work! We gonna do this?"

My team ended the day discussing the candidates. Since science teachers were a commodity, we agreed to call Mrs. Stout, candidate 3, back to meet with the superintendent as soon as possible.

I enthusiastically called her cell number. She answered

on the third ring. We discussed her next interview with the superintendent and confirmed a date and time to meet. She was more than thrilled!

It was one of those rare days when I headed home in a good mood before tapping into the wine reserves waiting for me in the dining room.

It's a nice night. Maybe a walk around the lake after Jeopardy! I thought.

CHAPTER 12

The Fort

June 22, 1964

I woke up at sunrise and had my usual extralarge bowl of cereal, 50 percent cereal, 50 percent sugar, a splash of milk, and my *Lone Ranger* silver spoon. It was then time for morning TV shows. *Mom's* shows.

Halfway through Jack LaLanne, my friends knocked on the back door.

"Hey, Joey! Do you have any nails?"

I nodded and wiped away my milk mustache. "What's up?" I asked.

"They're building a house at the vacant lot down the street. We dragged some two-by-fours and scraps of plywood into the woods behind Roger's house before the builders got there. We're gonna build a tree fort! Roger has some nails, but we need more."

"I got some," I said. Then I went into the basement and grabbed my dad's can of nails. I ran out the back door and hopped on my Schwinn.

We rode across the street through Roger's backyard to the edge of the woods. There, we picked out just the right tree to construct our fort in. It was a maple tree with thick, spread-out branches beginning six feet up. Perfect for easy access and spying! We began selecting two-by-fours and started nailing them into the tree independently from one another, knowing it would all come together in the end. I took no time at all to nail four two-by-fours, making a square frame around four sturdy branches. Once the frame was up, it was time to place the plywood on top for the floor and nail it onto the frame.

"We're out of nails," Roger said.

"How could we be out of nails? We had two cans full of 'em!" Micky shouted back.

We stepped back to look at our construction project. Yep, easily twelve nails used in every spot where two would have done the job. Time to hunt for more. Fortunately, the construction crew down the block was on lunch break. We snuck in and out, gathering as many dropped nails as possible to fit in our pockets. We then made our way back to the tree fort and continued construction.

We carefully attached the plywood floor to the frame and nailed in a safety rail that we knew couldn't even support a squirrel.

"Hey! We have four nails left!" I shouted.

Those we quickly hammered into the frame. Ya' know, for extra support.

Our masterpiece was complete. We looked at each other, then at the fort, then at each other again with pride. We sat on the plywood floor for the next half hour admiring our work and bragging about how it was the best fort ever built. No one could really see the fort, but we could see them … Perfect!

The sun was beginning to beat down through the trees so a few high fives later, we jumped off the fort and onto our bikes and headed to the town lake for a well-deserved dip.

The lake had always been our second home during the summer months since we were in first grade. To me, it was the lake. To my mom, it was the typhoid pit. On the way, we cut through the elementary school parking lot and saw two cars parked behind the building.

"Who in their right mind would want to be at school during the summer?" we joked. Then we continued to the lake.

We spent the rest of the afternoon diving off the high boards and swimming back and forth to the raft in the middle of the lake. Finally, with shriveled finger and toes, it was time to head home for dinner.

As Mom brought out the food, I told my family about the tree fort. Mom said she was wondering why there was so much hammering today between the new house being built and also coming from the woods. My dad smiled and nodded, while my brothers and sister just kept eating.

After a quick dinner, I met my friends at the end of the driveway where they were already waiting for me. And I thought I ate fast!

The sun was setting as we rode our Schwinns to the new house being built down the street. There was nothing like climbing around at a brand-new construction site.

We skidded our bikes on the gravel leading to the house. Once there, we scattered, but I was the first to jump onto the rusted, old, yellow tractor and began imagining myself clearing down the site. There was something about sitting on a tractor seat, shifting the gears, and gripping the steering wheel that gave us a sense of power. Especially when we hit the starter button and faintly heard a low growling noise that lasted about a split second.

The others started by climbing the frame of the house. This had already led to splinters in Peter's right hand and a nail puncture in Micky's left sneaker and slightly into his foot.

I joined in as we raced to the second level that had only a few floor sections nailed in. We hopped our way across the floor beams hoping not to slip through to the first floor. Keith did slip once but swung his arms around the floor beam, barely avoiding disaster. We, of course, laughed and tried to loosen his grip. He was not amused.

We then spotted a huge hole in the backyard with a big concrete tank in it that was shaped like a can of beans with holes all around it. We ran down and jumped on the tank, just missing the surrounding ditch.

"What do you think it is?" Micky asked, knowing we didn't know either.

We shrugged then lay down on our stomachs, bending over the edge trying to look in the holes, but all we could see was dark. The sun was almost set, which made it even harder to see.

There was a concrete lid on top that took all five of us to slide off to the side, exposing a hole about two feet wide. We looked down at more dark and shook our heads no.

"I'm goin' in!" Peter said.

We looked at him like he was out of his mind.

"You can't even see down there. Why would you want to go in?" I said.

"Why not?" he answered with an exaggerated courageous smile.

Keith agreed. "Don't do it! Let's get out of here. It's getting dark!"

"I bet you can't even fit through the hole anyway," Roger said in a voice coaxing Peter on.

"Oh yeah?" Peter shouted. "Watch this!"

Before we could say anything, Peter squeezed his way through the hole and slipped in. All we could hear was the echo of his sneakers hitting the bottom.

"See? I told ya'." Peter laughed.

Then there was silence ... Then more silence.

"Come on, Peter. Get outta there!" Roger said.

"Hey, guys? This is deeper than I thought. I'm a little wedged down here. Guys? ... *Guys?*" Peter said laughing but sounding really scared at the same time. "There's nothing to grab onto. *How do I get out of here?*"

We tried reaching in, but as Peter said, it was a little deeper than we thought. We looked for ropes or boards to lower down to him. We tried several things, but he couldn't grip on to pull himself out, and we couldn't balance from the top of the tank.

"Joey! Go get your brother, TJ! He's stronger!" Roger said.

I nodded yes then hoped on my bike and was gone. The sun was completely down now and with the darkness came the shouting of parent voices to get inside.

I ran in the house to get TJ. I tried to tell him what was happening, but I couldn't explain it for him to understand at first. But he followed me downstairs anyway.

"Come on! Just follow me. We have to get Peter out!" I said while pushing him to the door.

As we were leaving, my father stopped us. "Where are you going? It's dark out. Get in here," Dad said in a firm voice.

"We'll be right back, Dad. We just have to get something down the street," I answered, hoping he would just nod and walk by.

"Get in here!" he said louder and with a more irritated voice.

"But Dad, we gotta—"

"*What? We gotta what?*" he snapped back.

"Uhhhh ..." I started.

"Uh, *what?*" Dad said in a lower but more irritated voice. "*What?*"

"Ummm ..." I knew I had to say it or Peter would be down there all night!

"Peter's stuck in the ground at the house being built down the block," I said quickly while staring at the floor with my eyes squinting.

I looked up, and my father was already heading for the door. TJ and I followed.

Parents were at their doors waiting for Peter, Roger, Micky, and Keith to come home when they saw my dad heading down the street, with us close behind.

"Follow me!" Dad shouted to them.

They quickly joined the parade. Other curious neighbors followed, too. Another neighbor must have seen the commotion and called the cops!

In no time at all, there were crowds of neighbors surrounding the backyard of the new house. This was followed up with flashing dome red lights from two black-and-white police cars and a fire engine with its spotlights brightening up the entire property. My friends froze on the top of the tank, not knowing how this got so out of control. Micky put his hands in the air. Keith looked at him and just shook his head.

Officer Reed and his partner, Officer Malloy, ran to the back to analyze the situation. We told them what happened, and they immediately jumped on the tank. They aimed their flashlights down the hole, where they saw Peter standing at the bottom of this narrow cylindrical encasement barely able to move.

"You OK down there?" Officer Malloy asked.

Peter, way beyond embarrassed at this point, answered, "Yeah, I'm a little stuck and just can't get out."

We were standing off to the side with my father, completely overwhelmed but seeing the future humor in all of this.

Officer Reed got down on his stomach, reached deep down, and with a yank pulled Peter up. The neighborhood cheered. I imagine Peter just wanted to crawl back into the hole and disappear. His mother ran up and hugged him ... in front of everybody. He stood there, beet red, with glazed over eyes. I bet he was wondering if anyone would notice if he moved to Alaska.

We ran to Peter and patted him on the back then burst out laughing. But judging by the look on his face, I think he was wondering if this nightmare would ever be forgotten.

CHAPTER 13

The Assistant Principal

June 29

It a was already Thursday and we spent the past few days closing up pieces of the last school year. Prior to her 11:00 a.m. second interview with the superintendent, Mrs. Stout, our number 1 choice for the AP physics vacancy, called to politely inform us she would be taking a position with another district. In hindsight, I should have bet money on this. A teacher of her caliber must have had multiple offers before she even interviewed with us. It was not the first time this has happened, and I was pretty certain it wouldn't be the last.

Interviews continued for our other vacancies with special attention given to replacing my assistant principal. Previous candidates lacked the knowledge or experience for this position. Every school was different, and the staff selected should be able to relate to the students in the district. This didn't always equivocate to the experience or degrees an educator held but how they related with the students to have them learn. So far, no luck. We had a 2:00 p.m. interview with one last candidate before we enjoyed our well-deserved four-day weekend for the Fourth of July.

At 2:00 p.m. sharp, Ms. Frenzy guided a pleasant-enough-looking woman into the conference room. This time, she was not shaking her head, and as she exited the room, she gave a thumbs up!

The candidate was Reagan Cattlevic, a slight woman in her late twenties. Her references matched her resume and in-person interview qualities. She was calm, collected, intelligent, and direct. Her eye contact and pleasant smile, along with her breadth of educational knowledge, was that of a seasoned administrator. First impressions demonstrated to the search committee that she was not one to raise her voice when confronted with difficult situations. After a two-year break in service to take care of her elderly grandparents, she was more than ready to get back into the game.

When searching for an assistant principal, my personal preference was to find someone opposite of what I had to offer. I already had one of me. God knew I didn't need another one. I needed someone who could bring alternative views to the table in a professional and respectful manner.

Our standard interview questions became more conversational as Ms. Cattlevic was extremely engaging following up our questions with questions of her own. Not in a candidate sort of way but more collegial, as if we were already sitting in our administrative meetings with her. If I read the room correctly, this feeling was shared by the committee.

"Gotta move fast or were gonna lose this one," I texted Mrs. Keller. She slowly raised her thumb up as she read it. The others were reading our minds.

After the interview, I walked Ms. Cattlevic around the facility. She continued to be a comfortable conversationalist and asked all the right questions throughout the tour.

Reagan is just what the doctor ordered! I thought. *And she is available to start immediately.*

Realizing there was a board meeting next Wednesday evening, I tried to expedite the interview process with the superintendent and search committee. Fingers crossed. It looked pretty good. But you could never tell with this board.

CHAPTER 14

The Fourth of July Weekend!

July 4, 1964

Every year my parents would throw a Fourth of July barbecue in our backyard, and this year was no exception. TJ and I helped Dad bring the phonograph out to the driveway and set up the forty-fives under the old oak tree where they wouldn't melt. Dexie would be the disc jockey for the day, stacking five forty-fives at a time.

Mom supplied the hamburgers and hot dogs from the local butcher shop while the neighbors brought their specialty dishes. There was always corn on the cob, potato salad, coleslaw, tuna and macaroni salad, chips, dips, and a lot of beans. Dad had an ice chest for the Pabst Blue Ribbon, and Mom made the Kool-Aid. Grape flavor, of course.

Around one o'clock, the guests began to arrive. The moms and dads arranged the lawn furniture to be in groups, but also within earshot of all the conversations. There was the smell of freshly cut lawn mixed with the scent of Marlboros, Kents, and an occasional stogie in the air. The neighborhood kids ran wild everywhere the parents weren't while songs by the Beatles, Elvis, and an assortment of other artists played nonstop in the background.

It was a perfect sunny day that would last forever.

Around midafternoon, Dad dumped the charcoal briquettes into the brick barbecue grill. A few splashes of lighter fluid and a match or two later, and there was a flash of fire that could be seen from the lake. The black coals slowly began to turn a light gray as the heat built up around the grilling area. My dad knew just when to begin the cooking process. This was approximately two beers and a Kent or two later.

Once he flicked the butt of the Kent over the fence, the charcoals were perfect. It was time for Dad to add the hamburgers and hot dogs. We slowly gathered around the grilling area, waiting attentively, having built up quite an appetite from running around all afternoon.

After half a can of Pabst and a full Kent, followed by a few flips of the burgers and dogs and a lot more apron stains, my dad announced, "Dinner is served!"

A swarm of kids piled up plates with all the fixin's. My sister stacked up the Beach Boys on the Hi-Fi then joined the swarm. The adults, who were already four or five drinks into the afternoon, gathered around what was left, piled up their plates, then went back to their chairs. We ate anywhere we could find a place in the yard. Blankets, towels, the grass. It didn't matter.

While we were eating, we could hear the parents talking about us in competitive conversations. This included looking into our futures as police officers, milkmen, nurses, teachers, and secretaries. The conversation quickly changed to our schoolteachers and the school system.

"I heard one of the sixth-grade teachers just got engaged. I think it's Ms. Obdurate," Peter's mom said.

"I hope Joey gets her next year," my dad replied. "I think I saw her at the beach last week."

My stomach began to churn again. My understanding from numerous middle school kids was that Ms. Obdurate did things the old-fashioned way. She never changed or did anything fun like

the other teachers. You just sat in your assigned seat with your
hands folded on the desk and listened to her talk all day long.

"I hope so too," my mom added. "All the teachers are so nice
there."

"Steady," I whispered to myself.

Roger's mom said, "I think there's going to be a man teacher
this year. I don't know what grade, but I heard it at the grocery
store."

Much better! I thought.

The men shared a glance, smirked, and remained silent.

"I hope he can coach," Micky's dad finally said.

"Has anyone seen the principal lately?" Keith's mom asked.

Immediately they all burst into laughter.

I had had enough. Once our plates were empty, I shouted in a
commanding voice, "Who wants to play Jarts? I'll be a captain!"

All the neighborhood kids dropped what they were doing and
joined. Teams were formed with the usual boys against girls.

The object of the game was to toss the steel tipped Jarts into a
plastic circle placed on the ground by the other team. Much like
horseshoes. The neighborhood unwritten rules were to aim for the
other team without really hitting them. Even the parents laughed
when there was a close call. This lasted all of fifteen minutes until
we moved on to tag, climbing trees, trying to swing the highest
on the swing set, and of course a fight or two.

After a little more time passed, Mom shouted, "Watermelon!"

This was the main attraction followed up with cookies, cakes,
ice cream, popsicles, and more Kool-Aid.

The silence of enjoying our desserts and drinks was suddenly
interrupted by a thunderous explosion. Several of us spilled grape
Kool-Aid on our clothes. Others screamed. Neighborhood dogs
howled. My brother Bud began to whimper.

The parents burst out into laughter. Roger's father lit off a
cherry bomb!

Realizing we were OK, we ran to see more.

"I wanna light one!" "I wanna throw one!" "I'm the oldest. I go first!" could be heard coming from the small crowd of kids.

Roger's dad chuckled. "Easy, easy. Just sit back and enjoy!"

He continued to set off firecrackers one at a time. Then a string of 'em. When the sun started to go down, he lit off a few bottle rockets. While he was setting up for the finale of three Roman candles, an enormous explosion had all of us, including Roger's dad, hitting the deck! Everyone was covering their heads.

"Did the house explode? Did an airplane crash? Are we at war?" we all wondered.

All heads turned to my dad, who was laughing out of control. He took it a step up by lighting an M-80! We knew it was an M-80 because half of the grill was missing, and bricks were scattered all around the area. Everyone began to cheer, except my mother who stared at my father, then at the grill, then back at my father. Dad shrugged his shoulders and gave an innocent smile. He was in for it later, but it was worth it.

After things quieted down, Dexie managed to sneak a Pabst and two Marlboros by the parents. Right under their noses! As Dean Martin played over the evening crowd, all the kids gathered on the side of the house, hidden by forsythias and poison ivy. There we were giddy with anticipation. Each of us had what turned out to be two sips of beer and a drag of one of the cigarettes. Everyone, except for my older brother TJ. He would rather be a spectator than a participant. We played this for all it was worth, stumbling around and rolling our eyes convinced we were drunk. My kid brother Bud overexaggerated and wound up falling into the poison ivy. If anyone is super allergic to poison ivy, it's my fair-skinned kid brother Bud. It would only be a matter of time before my mom rolled out a keg of calamine lotion.

In the distance, the first fireworks could be heard from the high school fields. Everyone at the party gathered at the end our driveway, where the fireworks display could easily be seen. We sobered up fast ... or played the part anyway. That was our little secret.

I glanced down the street and could see that our higher numbered neighbors had the same idea as we watched and commented on each wonderful display of greens, blues, reds, and whites and the outrageous booms that resembled a rock drum solo with the typical ooohs and ahhhs. The show was great and lasted all of twenty minutes, finale and all.

My father lit off another M-80, bringing us to the ground once again.

"We could always replace that chunk of driveway," I said to Roger.

Mom wasn't amused. But having had her fair share of Blue Ribbon, the moment became a quick memory.

As the night went on, Peter's and Roger's fathers helped my dad light a bonfire. My mom and the other moms brought out the chocolate, marshmallows, and graham crackers. We collected sticks that Micky's dad whittled points on to skewer the marshmallows. My brother TJ preferred to place his stick directly into the hot coals burning the outside of the marshmallow. This flaming treat could easily be flicked at any number of unsuspecting targets. At this time of night, it would take a lot more than a flaming marshmallow skin to rattle the parents.

As we finished our treats, the dads lowered the clothesline that extended the length of the backyard to about four feet from the ground. The moms hung blankets and towels over the line for makeshift tents.

Within minutes of playing in the tents, we began to cozy up and fall asleep. The parents continued their drinking, smoking, and conversations until one by one they too drifted off to la-la land.

I remember waking up in the middle of the night to a few

empty tents and chairs. There were also a fair share of tenants still occupying their domains ... Best day ever!

Those of us who woke up at the crack of dawn went inside the house to watch Sunday morning cartoons and *The Sandy Becker Show*. Mom made coffee for any of the adults who braved the night.

Today would wind up being a blanket, couch, and recovery day of cartoons, the Yankees, and Ed Sullivan. It didn't get any better than that.

CHAPTER 15

The Fourth of July Weekend Down the Shore!

July 1–July 4

My wife and I headed down to our shore house for the long weekend. Our daughters and their families visited, but for the most part, they just hung around the pool all day. My wife and I preferred the beach.

We walked onto the sand and found our usual spot to settle in for the day. It was midmorning and there were only a few families scattered on the beach. We set up our chairs and blankets a few yards back from the water. Not five minutes later, a family of eight with a crying baby set up directly in front of us, tent and all, completely blocking our view of the ocean. Simultaneously, our neighbor Anthony set up shop two feet to the left of our chairs and lit up a Madura.

With smiles on our faces, we slowly slid our camp about twenty-five feet to the right. I guess that makes us twenty-five feet closer to Florida. I adjusted my pill speaker to a low volume and placed it on the blanket. Spotify was set to classic rock.

After a generous application of SPF 78 lotion, my wife began her eight hours of reading and solving word puzzles. I, on the other hand, began zoning out while staring at the waves. She would get up occasionally to take a dip in the ocean or when the ice cream guy, a Vietnam veteran, pushed the cart down the shoreline. She loved any flavored ice. As for me, it was always a Choco-Taco.

Although we were on a private beach, it was more crowded than usual with the Bennies and Shoobies celebrating the Fourth.

As the day went on, more people filled the beach and more individual and group conversations could be heard. And what do you think most of the talk was about?

"I quit my teaching job to work anywhere there's no kids or parents."

"I give all my students As. That way, my parents love me. It's like ... job security!"

"The trick is to give each class fifty math problems for homework every night. That way, you can spend half of the next day's class having your students go to the board and explain their answers. It's like teaching half a class!"

The next selection on Spotify was "Comfortably Numb" by Pink Floyd.

I focused on the waves ... Felt the waves ... Was the waves ... Other beachgoers said the following:

- "I give them a group project at the beginning of each marking period. We go to the media center every day. Gives me plenty of time to work out new plays for the football team. If you have a winning football team, you have a good school. Ask anyone how good they think another school is and it's always judged by how good the football team is. Prove me wrong!"
- "I have my doctor write me a note saying I have bad asthma and need to be in air-conditioning all day."

- "I can't wait for my kids to get out of that high school. I drop them off a half hour before school starts and they still get marked late because they're not in their home room on time ... Come on!"
- "Well, my daughter got suspended for fighting. A freshman was sitting where my daughter always sits in the cafeteria so she pushed her off." (That's not fighting. That's standing her ground. Right?)
- "Well, my son was sent out for a drug test Monday morning. The test came back positive. The school has no business interfering with what my kid does on the weekend. We go fishing, throw back a few, and smoke some pot. He's sixteen. I was twelve when my dad and I started. It's tradition!"
- "My kid brings his hunting knife to school. It makes him feel safe. If they have a problem with that, they'll have to go through me!"
- "Well, my f@%# daughter is always gettin' f@%# detention for swearing in school ... a@h@#s!"
- "I can't wait to get back to school in September. I'll be a senior and I miss my soccer coach. We're in love!"

Next selection was "I Wanna Be Sedated" by the Ramones.

Other beachgoers said this:

- "Did you ever notice the students' parking lot has nicer cars than the teachers' lot?"
- "Just tell 'em your kid's being bullied." Laughter. "Watch 'em jump." More laughter!
- "My daughter wants to be a teacher. I told her we're not going to have you live with us forever!"

- *"When's the marching band gonna get their own field?"*
- "My daughter has been taking gymnastics and dance lessons since she was two, and she didn't make varsity cheerleading? This school sucks!"

Next selection, "19th Nervous Breakdown," was by the Stones. A beachgoer said, "Is that Dr. Strat over there? I think it is! Let's say hello. He'll be so glad to see us. Maybe he'll tell us about our schedules for September! Make sure you video this for my podcast!"

The remainder of the holiday weekend wasn't much better. The quiet and private downtime my wife and I enjoyed coming to the beach took a 180. Everywhere we went, we would bump into teachers, parents, and students. Even during the fireworks display on the beach, we tried to keep our anonymity in the cloak of darkness, but with every burst of the rockets' red glare, the beach lit up to them waving and getting closer with their iPhones focused on us, recording our private downtime.

CHAPTER 16

Two-Week Summer Camp

July 6, 1964

Summer camp was an annual event in our town. It was held at the middle school, which was right next to the town library, for kids from first through eighth grade, 9:00 to 11:00 a.m., Monday through Friday, for two weeks. The younger kids were usually made to go, whereas we just went to meet up with other kids from town.

Roger, Keith, Micky, Peter, and I saddled up each morning and headed over, rain or shine. Our first stop was always the corner deli for Bazooka, sugar straws, and root beer Life Savers that we ate on our way there.

Once we got to camp, we parked our Sting-Rays in the overcrowded bike racks against the back of the school then walked in formation through the back parking lot to the gym. Kids were everywhere. Large groups of first and second graders were being dropped off by their mothers and neighbors. Some laughing, others hysterically crying and screaming. We walked around them to get into the building.

Everyone met in the lower bleachers of the gymnasium. The

few older kids who did show up gathered on the top corner where they could look down on us.

Once the last of the screaming first graders made their way in, a loud whistle quieted down the crowd. It was time for introductions that no one really paid attention to.

Every year, there were always the same three camp counselors who still didn't know our names or who we are.

Coach Blake was an eighth-grade English teacher in town. He was kinda young and had long, blond hair and a tan I'm pretty sure he was born with. He was holding a clipboard, a whistle, and a mug filled with coffee that read, "And That's The Way It Is" on its side.

Coach Clarkson was a retired policeman who lived in town by the ball field. He had a freshly cropped, flattop haircut and a thick, black mustache. He was wearing gray sweatpants and a white T-shirt with a picture of Cousin Brucie displayed on the front. Written below in blue letters was "WABC!"

Last but not least was Coach Lera. She was a retired gym teacher from the high school who had long, white hair and dingy, yellow teeth from smoking. She resembled the witch from *Snow White and the Seven Dwarfs*. Her cutoff T-shirt and tight, denim shorts were ... disturbing.

Coach Blake blew his whistle and shouted in a military voice, "Listen up! Pick an activity or sport. Go!" Then he blew the whistle again and was gone. That was the last we saw of Coach Blake, Coach Clarkson, and Coach Lera for the remainder of the camp. We were on our own.

Everyone went to different activities for the day. The younger kids ran to the arts and crafts tables that were covered with crayons, construction paper, paste, and leather cutouts of wallets and change holders that would be sewn together with leather twine. Some sat on the back stoop waiting for camp to be over, and then there were others who just ran around screaming for no reason at all.

Already one of the first graders was tasting the paste for texture and flavor. Others were chewing on the crayons.

My friends and I ran to the baseball fields where there was an odd combination of kids slowly gathering to play. Tommy, of course, was already on the pitcher's mound. That was his spot. With no adult supervision, Tommy was not only the pitcher but also coach, umpire, and equipment manager. He threw just the right pitches to the different age groups playing and always encouraged them with a smile.

Roger asked, "How do you think he does it?"

"I don't know what makes him so good," Peter answered.

Most of the kids didn't know how to play, but we got through at least two innings before we left.

The few older kids who showed up remained in the gym, where they sorted through Marvel and DC comic collections they brought from home. Dexie joined them mingling her collection with theirs. She really liked any kind of comic books. She also brought her prize transistor radio and cranked Herb Oscar Anderson, or HOA for short, on WABC all morning long!

Camp didn't last long, but we were used to going. It was a good warmup for the rest of the day.

CHAPTER 17

Getting into the Summer

July 6

Our Thursday morning meeting realized a more relaxed, and sunburned, staff.

Fortunately, everything worked out, and we were thrilled Ms. Cattlevic was approved at last evening's board meeting as our Ave Ridge High School assistant principal. They were unanimous in offering her the position. The sooner the better to get her on the team. If all went well, she would begin next Monday morning.

Naturally, we congratulated Mr. Minor on being released from his contract as of this Friday. The look of relief on his face was priceless. I'm confident Mr. Minor would be thrilled to begin his recovery—I mean new position—as soon as possible.

Coach Slick presented us with a new battle plan that included use of town fields. He was not happy, but it worked. We made a big deal about it because … Well, just because.

Next on the agenda was an update on scheduling. Being a smaller school, assigning special ed, AP, and honors courses intertwined with the other requirements was a monumental task. Singletons and the arts just made the process that much more difficult. Mrs. Keller had been laboring over this schedule since

February and hadn't gotten very far. She picked up some steam during June and July under extreme stress and pressure. Not everyone was cut out to be a scheduler.

Coach Slick insisted all in-house coaches had last period prep. The band director wanted last period prep to get the marching band out on the field early. The rest of the teaching staff also wanted last period prep ... just because.

Coach Slick then suggested trying a new scheduling approach. Straight eight periods with a block reserve for seniors and a three-day drop two for all students whose last name began with letters A through M, unless they were athletic freshmen not in the band. We stared in his direction, fascinated that this made sense to him.

I responded to this with as serious a face as I could without bursting into laughter. "I appreciate the out-of-the-box thinking on this, Coach! Why don't we all give it a good think while we consider all of the suggestions?"

I appreciated the fact that the others remained composed and nodded up and down as if this were a viable option.

I moved on quickly, changing the subject. "Who made the coffee today? It's awful," I said. "Tastes like bleach! See if one of the admin wants to make a Dunkin' run."

The meeting went on for another twenty-minutes with a lot of additional nothing getting done. I ended by giving all staff members their weekly assignments.

After the meeting was over, I went back to my office, where I was greeted by the board president, Mr. Dumass. He began with compliments on another great year and looked forward to the new school year. Then he got down to the business at hand.

His daughter, Precious, was involved in the girls' varsity soccer team. She was also on the town traveling league, was a member of the marching band, and wanted to be on the varsity cheerleading squad.

"There's not much you administrators do over the summer,

right? So how can you make this happen, Dr. Strat? I'm getting kickback from the coaches and advisors. Also, with her traveling so much, I would consider it a personal favor if her parking spot could be in the teachers' lot close to a locker at the end of the hall by the lot exit. We're planning a trip to Disney World for the first two weeks of September and would like you to do what you do to see she doesn't fall behind."

"I'll definitely get back to you once I've looked into each of your concerns, sir," I said, knowing the answers already. But to be fair, so did he.

"I know it's summer, so like I said, I'm guessing you don't have anything else to do. I'll check back with you next week. You like working here, don't you, Joe? See you then!" he said with a grin and a wave, then he was gone.

It was always a pleasure when the board president dropped by ...

I decided to skip lunch today and go to the county hospital to visit Mrs. Lass. Her surgery was two days ago so I thought I'd cheer her up ... and vice vera.

I walked into her private room quietly with flowers in hand. She looked pretty good and smiled when she saw me come in.

"You look wonderful!" I said. "How are you feeling?"

"Ahhh, I'm good. Gonna take more than this to keep me down," she said.

"So you're coming back tomorrow?" I said in a pleading wince with my fingers crossed.

She laughed. "Eight weeks and a lot of physical therapy."

She asked how things were going.

"You know," I said. "We're good."

We talked about office gossip, family, vacations, and the next school year. She was beginning to look tired so I cut the visit short. I always felt better after seeing Mrs. Lass. She could always brighten up anyone's day.

As I walked down the main corridor, I saw a few familiar

faces. Graduates of years gone by. It was good to see they were establishing careers in the health field. I was also surprised to see Mrs. Keller exiting the human resources office. We both seemed taken aback.

"Fancy seeing you here!" I joked. "Did you stop in to see Mrs. Lass?"

"No, umm. Actually. I was going to talk to you later. Oh, this is so awkward," she squeezed out.

She finally said, in a quick, monotone voice, "I just accepted a job here working on the psych ward. I'm sorry, Joe. I didn't want to tell you this way."

I stared at her, mouth open and dazed. I finally managed to say, "Whaaaaat?"

She continued. "The parents are driving me crazy. Nothing makes them happy. And with the scheduling and all … well, I feel the psych ward will be less stressful."

Again I managed, *"Whaaaaat?"*

I suggested we talk about this back at the office. She agreed.

Walking back to my car, I thought, *Directors of guidance are a dime a dozen …*

"S@&#! I'll never fill this vacancy!"

Once I got back to school, I saw that Mr. Minor's office was already bare and his desktop was loaded down with multicolored Post-it notes for Ms. Cattlevic. The look of relief on his face suggested he had an extra Lexapro, Valium, and Advil for lunch. No time to have what he was having. I had a 1:30 p.m. meeting with our district IT guy, Steve Jopps.

As Steve entered my office, he was already talking. "So Doc, remember all those smart boards we ordered for everyone and their brothers a few years back? Well, bulbs are out, screens are wearing, remotes are lost, yada, yada, yada."

I respond, "Do you mean those big, white things that cost us a fortune and took up three full professional development days and weekly department meetings to learn how to use interactively?"

"Uh, yeah," he said, sort of side-eye.

I continued. "And the same boards that only half the staff uses on any regular basis? And when they do use them, they might as well be using a $90 overhead projector?"

"Uhhhh, yeah," he repeated.

"And you want to do what with them now?" I said.

Steve stood up all excited with a huge grin on his face and his hands waving in front of him, preparing me for the chance of a lifetime. "Jamboards!" he shouted, changing to jazz hands.

In a mild raised voice, but with a forced smile, I said, "Are you kidding me? You want me to back another fad in technology that only a few will understand—or use for that matter—and will become antiquated faster than the smart boards? *Thousands and thousands of dollars?* How about we allocate $2,000 for some overhead projectors until you can show me some solid data or any evidence that we even need them."

With a little less enthusiastic jazz hands and a forced grin, he replied, "Whatta ya' say to fifty thousand and we give it the old Ave Ridge try?" Both his thumbs were now straight up next to the growing smile on his face.

"Out!" I shouted and pointed to the door.

"But—"

"*Out!*"

Before the door could close behind him, in strolled Mrs. Keller with her official letter of resignation.

"Please don't hate me, Joe!"

"I don't hate you," I replied.

"I promise I'll stay for my sixty days. I'll even work with my replacement if you want me to. Just don't hate me!" she said through a troubled smile.

With that, she scurried back to her office and shut the door behind her. Lights off, shade down.

I reached for my phone and called my pal, Tommy. "How was your day?" I asked.

Tommy mumbled on the other end.

"Uh huh. Me too," I continued.

More mumbling came from Tommy.

"I'll meet you there. First round is on me!" I said while exhaling.

"How many more years till retirement?" I asked myself. "The days are all blurring together."

When I arrived to work the next morning, Friday, I saw that all of our office furniture was stacked in the hallway. Mrs. Keller was belly crawling across the desktops and file cabinets. Mr. Minor was just shoving stuff out of the way. Iggy and his men stared and grinned as they slurped down their first coffees of the morning.

"Change of plans, Doc," Iggy said. "Coach Slick rearranged his indoor practice schedule. This is the only time we can do this area."

At the very end of the main corridor, I saw Coach Slick smiling, waving, then shrugging his shoulders. "Sorry," he said as he turned toward the gymnasium doors while laughing.

We worked our way through the obstacle course to our empty offices and gathered our laptops that were stacked randomly on the main office countertop then moved our operation to the media center.

During our morning briefing, Mr. Minor played solitaire, knowing this was his last day, while Mrs. Keller kept hinting at the number of vacation and sick days she had accumulated. So after the meeting was over, I spent the remainder of the morning networking across the state hoping to find a replacement for her. The state principal/supervisor association was very helpful guiding me with several leads.

It was just before lunch when Ms. Sharp, the administrative assistant for guidance, gave her sixty-day notice. It seemed she and Mrs. Keller worked so well together that she also got a job in the psych ward at County Hospital.

I asked myself why I didn't become an accountant like my father.

Being Mr. Minor's last day, I'm surprised he came in at all. We took him to lunch at Jazzy's, where we roasted him mercilessly, presented him with a few tokens of our appreciation, and threw back a few drinks. The superintendent, Harriet Fieldman, joined us for the festivities.

Mr. Minor gave a very impassioned speech thanking everyone who had helped him along his career path. As he graciously continued, his voice grew softer and softer and then his right eye began to twitch uncontrollably. He reached in his pocket for four Advil, popped them in his mouth, and washed them down with straight bourbon. This was followed by a glance around the room and a slight smile as he sat down saying, "Yeah, I made the right move. I'll miss you guys, but ... yeah ... yeah ..."

His right hand continued to shake as he held on to the empty glass. Harriet and I locked eyes. I nodded then she nodded back signifying I would have the pleasure of driving Mr. Minor home while she followed me driving his car back.

CHAPTER 18

Summer Cuts and the Movies

July 10, 1964

Mom piled my brothers and me into the car Friday morning to take us for our summer haircuts. It was a short ride to the north end of town on Main Street where we parked in the small lot in front of a long row of stores.

Tony's Barbershop was squeezed in between Bernardo's Record Store on the left and Maria's Pizza Parlor on the right.

Mom led the way past the spiraling red, white, and blue pole and into the shop to see if there was a time for us, somewhere. There were two barber chairs with only one barber wearing a bright white jacket. His small appearance included a big personality. That and an enormous mustache, thick, black, rimmed glasses, and a slim, gold watch.

Tony answered, "Hello, Mrs. Strat! It's always good to see you and the boys. They're getting so big, huh? Of course, there's time for you. There's always time for you! I just finished up Telly and Yul. Your boys are next."

"So Tony! I have a few errands to run. You know how the boys' hair is cut, right? I'll be back in about fifteen minutes. You let me know if they give you any trouble."

"These are good boys. No trouble, Mrs. Strat. No trouble," Tony said with a smile and a mild shoo away gesture. "You go. We'll be good."

When the two other gentlemen left, Tony patted down the barber chair looking at my brother Bud.

"You're first!" Tony said with a smile.

Bud hopped onto the chair as Tony wrapped him in a large, brown cape and combed his hair straight back. Before Bud could say a word, the buzzers were fired up and ready for action. Tony went from the front center of Bud's head right through to the back of his neck. Bud's eyes bulged out.

"But I wanted a—" Bud was cut off.

"Oh, no buzz cut this time?" Tony asked.

TJ and I locked eyes, then laughed uncontrollably.

"Can ya' fix it?" TJ joked.

"TJ!" Bud shouted, almost ready to cry.

It took a while trying to convince Bud he would look great! The buzz cut was definitely his style. Even Tony agreed. We all shared an awkward look then turned to Bud.

"Well, can't do much about it now. Might as well," Bud said, a little more optimistically.

Tony continued shaving down Bud's melon in about three seconds flat. He took out that huge brush loaded with talc and brushed off his head like he was cleaning home plate. The cape came off, the seat brushed down, and with that pleasant smile, Tony said, "*Next?*" looking directly at me.

I cautiously walked over to the chair. Bud was already sitting next to TJ, both feeling his buzzed head like it was an unhatched egg.

Before I sat in the chair, Tony and I would have a conversation. "Hi, Tony!" I began. "Just trim up the bangs and sides. No whitewalls, OK?"

"But I always buzz around the ears. You look handsome for your mom, huh?" Tony replied.

"Let's just try it my way first. I'm going into middle school in September so I need to change a few things, OK? Ya' know, just trying something different is all," I said.

Smiling brightly he said, "OK, OK, OK, we try it."

First, he cut the bangs high enough so I could see followed by trimming around the ears, leaving enough hair hanging over to look less … elementary school. He trimmed the back, but not too short.

"This is the way kids wear it now, huh?" Tony said, again with a big smile.

"That's it, Tony! Thanks!" I said while hopping off the chair. Tony followed me with the talc and smacked it across my neck.

"Gottcha!" He laughed.

After cleaning down the chair and shaking out the cape, he said, Next!" while staring straight at TJ.

TJ got up and walked toward the chair. He shook Tony's hand and said in a matter-of-fact way, "Just a trim. I'm letting it grow." He sat down and adjusted to make himself comfortable.

"You're mama good with this?" Tony asked with a little less of a smile, a tilted head, and a raised right eyebrow.

"I'm going into high school. Gotta be one of the guys, right?" TJ answered. He then folded his arms under the cape, closed his eyes, and relaxed for the haircut.

Just then a bell rang as the door to the shop opened. It was Mom. Tony smiled and dropped his arms to his sides.

She looked at Bud and shouted, "How adorable!"

Bud smiled but turned red at the same time. Our laughing didn't help.

She looked at my hair, stared a second, then said, "Where's that clean-cut boy with the whitewalls?"

"I'm older now, Mom. It looks good, right?" I said with a forced smile.

Mom looked at Tony, who was already nodding yes. My mom started nodding yes as she looked back at me and said, "Yes, yeah! It looks good!"

I felt older already.

"Now," my mother continued, "don't tell me you're done, TJ."

"No, no, Mrs. Strat! We were just about to begin when you came in."

"Oh! So what are we doing, TJ?" Mom asked.

"Gonna let it grow, like my friends. You know, like Paul McCartney," he said with a smile and a wink.

Mom thought for a moment, smiled, then gave the OK for Tony to begin.

When all three of us were done, Mom handed over $4 and told Tony to keep the change. We left the barbershop just as a line was forming with other families getting their beginning of summer haircuts too!

On the short drive home, all three of us were rubbing the back or our necks, trying to get rid of the itchy feeling of the leftover cut hair that the brush and talc missed.

When we got home, my friends were waiting at the end of the driveway. It was getting hotter out so we decided to ride our bikes to the movie theater one town over. It only took twenty minutes, and the matinee started at 1:00 p.m. Today it was a double feature with *Pink Panther* and *A Hard Day's Night* with two cartoons at the beginning for only $1.25. It was a great way to spend the afternoon.

We entered the theater foyer, and it already felt cooler as we opened the door then paid for our tickets. Our next stop, of course, was to head for the snack counter. The same high school kid who sold us the tickets also worked the snack stand. There was a pretty good selection so we got quite an assortment.

To enter the main theater, there was a center aisle that inclined. The rows of seats were facing us on both sides. The huge screen was overhead and behind us. The theater had seen better days but was comfortable by our standards. You could always count on having your sneakers stuck to the carpet on the way to your seat. Choosing the best seat depended on how much gum was stuck to the bottom when it was in the up position and how much sugar candy and popcorn butter residue was on the torn cloth seat when in the down position. Ultimately, the final decision depended on how much the center spring in the seat had worked its way to the surface. Duct tape could only cover so much.

Large propeller fans surrounding the dark theater kept us cool compared to the summer heat outside. We chose our seats on the left, dead center, and began to share a bucket of buttered popcorn, Juicy Fruits, and some Cokes. The only other people in the theater were my brother TJ and his friends, who monopolized the back row doing the same.

Movies during the week were awesome because there was hardly anyone there. We had run of the place. The high school kid who sold us the tickets and snacks took his place in the projector room and started the first cartoon. From that point on, he phoned it in.

The movies were good, and the three and a half hours went by fast. Much better than being at school. It was great seeing a movie on the big screen and in color compared to the black-and-white Zenith back home.

It was 4:40 when the movies let out, so we biked home just in time for dinner where my dad already had the charcoal grill heating up with hot dogs and beans. My favorites!

We ate outside under the trees where it was still hot, but much cooler than in the house.

Mom turned the lawn sprinkler on and it swept back and forth over the backyard. We all took random runs through it, while Dad pulled his chair directly into the water zone, covering his Pabst each time the water swept by.

After dinner, my friends joined us in the backyard to cool off. Once Mom and Dad went inside, we tried to remember jokes the older kids told us at the movie theater that they heard on *The Benny Hill Show*.

The rest of the weekend came and went. Then it was back to camp.

CHAPTER 19

Ms. Cattlevic

July 10

I arrived half an hour early this Monday morning, knowing it was Ms. Cattlevic's first day. The office was cleaned and the furniture was moved back in ... sort of.

Ms. Cattlevic was already in her new office getting settled. I greeted her with a coffee from Dunkin' and asked how her weekend was. Following some small talk, I suggested she get settled in and that our first staff meeting would begin at 10:00 a.m. in the conference room. She thanked me again for the opportunity to work here then continued unpacking her laptop, and two boxes of papers and pictures for her desk and walls. As the rest of the staff arrived, each of them stopped by her office with a smile to welcome her to the team.

For the next hour or so, I compiled the game plan for this week's agenda. It was a great start for a Monday morning.

Twenty minutes before the meeting, Mrs. Sycoe made her second appearance of the summer as she burst into the main office with her son Sidney. Her first appearance on June 23 concluded with her realizing and confirming that Sydney had to go to summer school for gym. She already began her rant in the hallway.

"This school sucks! Sidney is in danger of failing summer school and it's not his fault. Just because ..."

I heard her. I saw her through my office window. I wasn't quick enough.

Ms. Cattlevic came out of her office to see what all the commotion was. "Hi, I'm Ms. Cattlevic. Can I help you?" she said in a calm voice and a smile on her face.

"Ms. *Cattle* ... Really?" Sidney mocked.

"Shut up, Sidney," Mrs. Sycoe said. Then she shouted even louder, "*Who the hell are you?*"

Before I could run interference, Ms. Cattlevic invited them both into her office. Her window shade was up as she closed the door, but we couldn't see in because of the angle. We all froze. The next few minutes seemed like an eternity. All that could be heard was Mrs. Sycoe ranting.

I thought, *She doesn't even have a coffee maker set up in her office yet!*

Coach Slick entered the main office with a spring in his step, whistling the Notre Dame fight song. When he glanced into Ms. Cattlevic's office, his face went pale. I'd never seen such a frightened expression from such a tough structure of a man. He looked at each of us confused, stammered incoherently, then left the office quickly and ran back to the gym.

Iggy and his crew gathered in the hallway just outside of the main office pretending to clean. This was big doin's and they weren't going to miss out.

Clouds thickened outside. Thunder could be heard in the distance. Dogs barked. Birds flew off the trees and power lines. The office staff was horrified, yet none of them could gather the strength to go to her aid. Ms. Sharp clutched her purse and appeared to be praying.

"She's so young!" someone said.

The tension was unbearable and still kept building. A police cruiser passed through the parking lot. Word traveled fast in a small town.

I'd been in this situation numerous times throughout my career and knew exactly what to do. I sat behind my desk and began writing the ad for an assistant principal vacancy.

Suddenly there was an uneasy silence ... Nobody moved. More silence ... I reached for my phone to dial 911.

Just then, Ms. Cattlevic opened her office door. We waited ...

Ms. Cattlevic guided Mrs. Sycoe and Sidney out of her office. All three of them were smiling.

She looked back at them and said, "It was a pleasure meeting both of you. Call me anytime if I can be of further assistance."

Mrs. Sycoe said in a calm friendly voice, "Thank you, Ms. Cattlevic. Sidney won't let you down."

Sidney added, "It was nice to meet you, Ms. Cattlevic," as the two Sycoes left the building.

At that exact moment, the sun shone through the windows, forming what seemed to be a halo over Ms. Cattlevic's head.

"She's a keeper!" I whispered for anyone in earshot range to hear.

Everyone remained still. All eyes were on Ms. Cattlevic, who looked around at us smiling and said, "What? What did I miss?"

The staff burst into cheers, laughter, and applause. From this moment on, Reagan was a full-fledged member of our team.

When the commotion finally died down, I reminded everyone of our 10:00 a.m. meeting.

All eyes stared my way.

I stood tall and firm then said, "OK, 10:30 a.m."

More cheers.

We gathered around the conference table at 10:30 a.m., still feeling the energy from this morning's episode. The first item on today's agenda was formally introducing Ms. Cattlevic as our new assistant principal. In a shy, mild-mannered tone, she assured us she would be available for whatever needed to be done. She then turned her attention back to me to continue with the agenda items. For the first time this summer, I felt like there was hope.

"Today we need to focus on transfer students and how they will affect our class sizes," I continued.

Mrs. Keller slipped me an envelope addressed to our guidance department from Our Lady of Stealum High School requesting the records for upcoming freshman Luke Champion.

Luke was an all-star athlete, first chair saxophone player in the concert band, and academic overachiever—the freshmen class trifecta!

"We train 'em, they beat us with our own feeder system," I said.

It was truly disheartening to educate students pre-K though grade eight in any sport, academic area, or the arts when they got recruited by a private high school. When you got beaten by an athletic team made up of kids you trained for years but were now competing against you as freshmen and beating you, try to explain that to board members when they want the coaches replaced. Or when the academic scores come out and the state credits the students you trained to the private school.

Interestingly enough, I had three nuns in my family. My aunt and godmother was a cloistered nun. My great aunt was a parochial high school principal, and my second cousin was an elementary parochial school principal. They all told me the same thing. "Not all nuns go to heaven." I got it!

"Oh, he's not the only one." Mrs. Keller continued. "There are seven more. All top students in academics, athletics, and the arts."

This was what I referred to as "acaleticarts." The three As for success.

It was not an easy task to explain to the board why we were not considered a top-rated high school. I could present charts, graphs, data, and even tape test scores and results to the side of a six-pack. But when you trained the students from pre-K through eighth grade then saw them recruited to the private and parochial schools, with scholarships, it was disappointing. Especially when not one board member's child had been recruited.

Oddly enough, if you charted the students who had started in our district as preschoolers and gone through to the eighth grade, we weren't doin' bad.

Mrs. Keller also informed us that a family of six, with four high school students, would be moving into the district. All four students would be out-of-district placements.

I thought, *I'm losing hope that there is hope.*

The last agenda item was to adjust the phone directory to include new hires throughout the summer. My specific directive was to relocate the principal's name and number to twenty-six on the voicemail menu. I further requested that my email address and phone extension be taken off the web site contact information page. After all, if the issue was really important, they would call the main number. Or they would have my cell number. Or … I dunno. Just have Mr. Jopps put me last on the list.

CHAPTER 20

A Rainy Summer Day

July 13, 1964

It was a rainy Monday morning, but we rode off to camp anyway. Many of the younger kids were missing. The older kids were soaking wet sitting on the top bleachers. Tommy tried to convince everyone that playing baseball in the rain was a tradition! No takers. So instead we had three options.

1. Make a leather wallet.
2. Hang out in the bleachers and dry out.
3. Make our way into the school hallways without getting caught.

Option 3 it was!

This was the middle school we would be attending in September so we might as well become familiar with the layout now! The trick was to get past the coaches' office that led to the main hallway.

Tommy opted out by saying, "I hate school during the year. Why would I want to go in it during the summer?"

"Come on, Tommy. It'll be fun!" Keith said.

"Nah … See ya' later," Tommy said as he ran up the bleachers to join the older kids.

"See ya' later," we said back.

Roger took the lead and walked slowly and lightly as he approached the coaches' closed office door on the left. Craning his head, he peeked into the office window. Relieved, he stood straight up, turned, and waved us on. He then skipped past the office.

We were cautious entering the danger zone, but Roger said it was safe, so one by one we treaded lightly as we passed the window. But then, we also just walked normally to the main hallway.

As we individually peeked in, we could see Coach Blake and Coach Clarkson with their backs to the door, watching *I Love Lucy* on a small RCA TV. Coach Lera was slumped over her desk face down and fast asleep with nothing but long, white hair hanging off the edges. We made it past the first obstacle.

Next we had to lift the locked hallway gate just high enough to slide underneath without getting stuck. One by one we GI Joe'd our way through, leaving wet streaks from our soaked jeans and shirts on the floor. Home free!

We ran up the stairs to our right, busting through the double doors into a network of hallways. We each headed in a different direction. The hunt was on. No one needed to know the rules of the game; it just developed as it went along.

All that could be heard through the hallways were running footsteps, wet sneaker screeches, laughing, the banging of lockers, and then more running.

We finally met up on the opposite side of the building, not really sure of our way back so we ran down the nearest staircase.

Just before opening the double doors, Peter blocked us and whispered, "Stop!"

We all peeked through the double door windows and saw an old man moving a desk through the hallway.

"What's he doing here?" I whispered. "It's summer. No one goes to school in the summer."

Another older man and woman joined him moving desks down the hallway.

"What are we gonna do? They're blocking our way out," Micky said.

We all looked at each other for guidance ... Nothin'.

We came up with a plan. When they got down the hallway, we would sneak through the doors and go to the right.

A few seconds later, Roger said in a low, determined whisper, "We'll go on three. Wait for it ... One, two, three. Go! Go! Go!"

We swung open the doors and hung a hard right. As we began to pick up speed a voice called out, "Stop!"

Standing directly in front of us was a fourth elderly janitor. Peter and Roger started to run again. Micky, Keith, and I stopped. Micky, Keith, and I started to run again. Peter and Roger stopped. We turned to go back and ...

"Stop!" the voice said again, a little louder this time.

We did.

"Ohhhhhh ... This is not good," I said in the direction of my future cell mates.

The janitor tilted his head with a stern look on his face and asked, "What are you doing here?"

In a quiet and confused voice, Keith asked, "What are you doing here? School's closed!"

"I'm Chuck, the head janitor. How do you think the building gets cleaned? You kids left it a mess on the last day."

"Are you going to call the police on us?" I asked. "We can just go. Nobody has to know we were here. Really!"

"Why shouldn't I?" Chuck said as a slight smile began to show on his face. "Do you kids go to school here? I don't remember seeing you."

"We'll be going here in September. We'll be in sixth grade. We just ... got lost ... from camp," I said.

"Yeah, yes, uh huh!" the others joined in.

"So you got lost with the locked gate down, huh?" Chuck smirked.

By now, the other three janitors circled around us, listening in to our story. They smiled and nodded to each other, making believe what we were saying was true.

"You're lucky the principal didn't catch you. That wouldn't be a good start to your middle school years," another janitor said.

"That's Barry," Chuck said.

I said, "You know, that sounds a lot like—"

"We know!" they responded in unison.

"Why would the principal be here? It's the summer!" Keith asked in the same quiet and confused voice.

"You got a lot to learn about stuff," Barry said. The other janitors nodded in agreement.

"So can we go now?" I asked in a semipleading voice.

The janitors glanced back and forth at each other. They seemed to be communicating without talking.

Chuck looked us in the eye and pointed to the open classroom doors. "You see those four classrooms?"

We all nodded, trying to understand what he was getting at.

"Well," he continued, "if you boys move all of the desks and books out of those classrooms and down to the end of the hallway before the principal gets back, we'll give you each a dollar. But you can't tell anyone or the deal is off! Deal?"

Chuck extended his hand.

Before it was fully extended, we shouted, "Deal!" in unison.

For the next forty-five minutes, the janitors smoked cigarettes and drank coffee as they watched us work. We were sweating, but we were getting paid!

When the last desks and books were in place, Chuck gave us

each a dollar bill and guided us back through the building to the gate. He unlocked it to let us back into the gymnasium where camp was still going on.

As we each exited through the gate, he said, "Don't forget our deal!" then winked at us as we headed back to the bleachers to join the others.

CHAPTER 21

Summer Curriculum Development

July 13

Today, the curriculum committee would meet for one of three summer curriculum development days. It was made up of one teacher from each of the core content subject areas and electives who showed an interest in curriculum development and, more importantly, an interest in the stipend.

The three professional development days would be rich with research of scope and sequence, unpacking standards, cutting and pasting, plagiarizing—uhh, that is *sharing of materials,* and binding of the final product for approval by the board of education.

These curricula would be labeled by department and subject then bound in school-colored binders. Once approved by the board, they would be ready for distribution to each subject area teacher along with assessment rubrics for desired outcomes. The teachers would receive the approved curriculum binder that they would use as an outline for the entire school year for vertical and horizontal articulation. Or in the real world, the staff would sign a document that they received the curriculum binder that they would then lock in a safe place. Hopefully, they would be able to find it to hand in at the end of the school year.

Throughout the years, I had seen new strategies, studies, rubrics, mandates, trainings, unpacking, and reassessments of curriculum designed to address the needs of the individual learner. It got more and more difficult each year. Meanwhile, unless an administrator did his or her due diligence, curriculum would be whatever the teacher did once they closed the classroom door.

English

Forget the assigned reading from the curriculum ... The teacher would find a novel they liked better. This changed as the year went on.

Science

Textbook? An experiment a day. What did the budget allow? Just have the students bring in rubber bands, empty milk containers, old CDs, electric fan motors, etc. The rest of the time would be utilized showing reruns of *How It's Made*.

Social Studies

Whatever sport season it was, the teacher/coach would determine the type and length of the marking period project to be assigned.

Band Director

Teaching instruments by rote to put on a good public performance to wow the parents. Music history? Music theory? Naaahh ... Rote. Parents wanted to hear their kids playing recognizable songs. Like Harold Hill did in *The Music Man!*

Art/ Photography

The art/photography teachers would spend most of their budget on picture frames so their students could wander the hallways taking pictures of anything and everything! With that being said, the pictures were surprisingly good.

Health and Physical Education

Keep the students in the gymnasium or on the fields.

When I arrived as principal, our health and physical education curriculum was delineated with all the current standards, methodologies, including written assessments. Following the first few walk-throughs and informal observations, it was apparent the students were just going through the motions of what they had been doing since first grade. The only difference was that of the four assigned teachers, one was selected to watch all of the students each period on a rotating basis. The other three would prepare for their after-school sports.

Math

Our math curriculum was designed for the three students in the front row who could actually keep up with what the teacher was presenting.

Choral Director

Sing. Let the students sing.

Our last choral director worked endless hours for individual and ensemble lessons and rehearsals to present *Carmina Burana* by Carl Orff for the spring concert. This was aligned to the curriculum. It involved difficult harmonization, challenging syncopations, ear training, posture, breath support, timbre, and self-tuning, to name only a few. The choir practiced before and after school and during lunchtime and attended several night rehearsals.

The day of the spring concert arrived. For those in the audience who appreciated fine musical literature, iPhone screens were lit up to record the talent of the director and all the students in the choir. For the others, their iPhone screens were lighting up their faces as they scrolled through social media, texted, checked email, and sent the newest emoji to their friends.

At the end of the selection, there was average applause.

At the following board meeting, several members were questioning if the choral director was the right person for the job.

One member commented, "They didn't sing one song I knew." Others nodded in agreement.

"Our last director had them sing all the newest popular songs," another said.

I remember my head dropping down with my eyes closed while thinking, *The last director had the entire choir singing in unison. It took one week to prepare, and the students learned absolutely nothing!* But the crowd loved the show!

Special Education

Students would be able to recognize the following:

- Their teacher was their biggest advocate.
- Their teacher would adjust all academic and life lessons so their students would succeed.
- Their teacher would volunteer to attend all functions their students were involved in for support and backup.
- Their teacher would be there for them many years after they graduated.

Required Professional Development

- how to verbally sedate unappreciative parents
- educating the administration and board on district special education needs while making them think they thought of it themselves
- controlling the impulse to spend your entire paycheck on supplies for your students

Computer/Technology

Try to keep up with the students!

CHAPTER 22

The Last Day of Camp

July 17, 1964

The last day of camp was a free-for-all. We were reintroduced to the summer staff who took several pictures of the groups to post on the bulletin boards for all the board members to see. They then disappeared back into their offices until dismissal, where they wished us a safe summer and shook hands with the few parents who dropped off and picked up their kids each day.

At one point, we saw the janitors on break having cigarettes and coffee in one of the classrooms at the end of the wing. They looked out the window, saw us, waved, and smiled then went back to their conversations. It left us with a good feeling. They remembered us.

An hour later and camp was closing for the summer. Our mission was clear. We wore baggy sweatpants so we could each take home as many baseballs as we could fit in our clothes without the coaches catching on. We managed eleven balls all together. Tommy managed to take first and second base and a whistle from one of the coaches!

CHAPTER 23

Not the School Nurse!

July 14

It was Friday morning and I had called a meeting with our medical suite coordinator, Nurse Chapel. She was contracted to come in twice a month over the summer to get the medical records updated and calendar the various student exams given throughout the year. She had been the school nurse for the past thirteen years and was well respected by the students, staff, and community.

Yesterday, I received a letter from a concerned parent.

> Dear Dr. Strat,
>
> A few of my neighbors have been talking about the upcoming school year and we would like to make you aware of a potential situation.
>
> My son, Randle, has been taking Ritalin over the past two years that Nurse Chapel administers at lunchtime each day. I have noticed over the past year that we periodically have come up short on pills. I'm certain I correctly count each month,

but when Nurse Chapel contacts us, I send her whatever is needed.

It seems the other mothers have been experiencing the same issue. This has never happened before, and I don't want to get Nurse Chapel in any kind of trouble. It just seems odd that we would all be experiencing the same thing.

Please call me so we can discuss this matter further.

Sincerely,

Mrs. Gladys Kravitz

Nurse Chapel entered my office wearing jeans and a lab coat. She brought both of us coffee and began telling me about the Fourth of July weekend at her sister's house in Cape Cod. After the pleasantries, I asked her to read the letter. Her face dropped and her eyes shifted toward the door.

"I don't understand. Why would she write a letter like this?" Nurse Chapel said in a low, wavering voice.

"I don't know," I answered. "What do you think it's about?" I looked at her directly to make eye contact.

She continued to look toward the door.

"Joe, you know me. I think maybe she and her friends were having a few drinks and began exaggerating. You know how parties can get. I'll look at my records. I'm sure there's a logical explanation," she said.

"Are you sure you counted correctly? Maybe you dropped a few pills? Mixed up bottles?" I suggested.

"That's never happened before, but maybe I … Well, I guess it's possible. You know. It gets pretty hectic down there at lunchtime and … I dunno. Maybe," Nurse Chapel was visibly shaking.

Still no eye contact.

"Christine, look at me. Is there something you're not telling me? I know you confirm the count on all medications the parents send in," I nudged.

Still not looking me in the eye, she responded, "Well, this has never happened before and … What I mean is … I know there's records, and—"

"Christine? Level with me."

"I can't! I'm not ready for this! It's not my fault!" she shouted.

"What's not your fault, Christine? Christine?" I persisted.

Christine started to cry. "You don't know what it's like! You just don't know what it's like day in and day out! Home, work, my kids, my pets, shopping, making dinner … It never ends! I'm always just so tired! I just need a little help, ya' know? I didn't think it would get out of control so fast! It makes me feel like I could get through the day! Please don't tell anyone. Joe, Joe, I promise I'll stop. I promise! … Sh@&!"

I tried so hard to keep my face neutral. Christine was a wonderful, dedicated nurse and friend. And addicted to drugs? She just lost everything. It made me sick to think that as a mandated reporter, I was going to have to call the police.

"Christine," I answered with a sympathetic voice. "How long has this been going on?"

"Christine? … Christine?" I repeated.

Still no answer as she stared down at her hands.

"Christine, I'm trying to understand. I want to help you," I said in a concerned tone.

Still no answer.

I continued. "I'm afraid I have to let the superintendent know. You know that's procedure. You know what both of us have to do."

"Pleeeease, Joe. Please!" she cried.

"Christine, please listen. You'll get through this. But I also can't let you drive so we'll have to contact your husband to pick you up."

"Joe!" she pleaded, this time looking me straight in the eyes. "I'm begging you. Please! My family, my career!"

"But first you're going to have to talk to Harriet and Captain Pike from the police department," I said in a steady but disappointed voice.

"Am I gonna lose my job?" she asked, still sobbing. "Joe? Joe, please … Please … Please, Joe. Please!"

I called Mrs. Keller into the office without letting Christine out of my sight. Christine was sobbing uncontrollably while Mrs. Keller tried her very best to calm her down.

Moments later, the superintendent and Captain Pike joined us. Nurse Chapel admitted to taking the students' medication and was taken down to the police station, where her husband met her.

I sat in my office staring at the wall for the next half hour. The remainder of the day, I shuffled around some papers with the door closed. The last thing I did before leaving was to post for a school nurse vacancy.

CHAPTER 24

Mastering Wheelies!

July 18, 1964

We all got up early for a Saturday morning. We had no plans but met at the end of my driveway anyway just to ride our bikes around.

Riding our bikes in circles was just a warmup. Pedaling fast past a few houses then jamming on the back breaks so the rear of the bike would skid in circles leaving tracks came next. Then there was a combination of standing on our banana seats and making S patterns on the road, followed by pedaling with no hands and finally jumping the curbs.

Looking up the block to the higher numbered houses, we could see the older kids popping wheelies on their Sting-Rays with the extended forks they recently installed.

"That's easy," I said in a mocking way.

"Ppfffssssttt, you know it!" Roger said while rolling his eyes.

Keith, Micky, and Peter stuffed some more Bazooka into their mouths and nodded in agreement.

We started mimicking the older kids by pulling the front end of our bikes up while pedaling fast. One by one we found ourselves sprawled out on the street with our bikes lying next to us.

"Watch me! I can do this!" I said confidently.

I got up, brushed myself off like in the cartoons, picked my bike up, and began to pedal. I could feel all eyes on me as I gained speed. I leaned forward then yanked the monkey bars back with all my might.

The next thing I remembered was lying on the street flat on my back with my prize Sting-Ray two doors down against a pile of rusted garbage cans. I was in pain, but this wasn't stopping my friends from laughing hysterically. I looked around for a hand to help me up ... Not a chance. I went to retrieve my bike while wiping off the bloody scrapes on both of my elbows.

It was Roger's turn. "Watch how it's done, lllooosssers!" he said while pumping his pedals hard to gain speed. Faster, faster, front dip, then he pulled back hard and ... I'd never seen a body twist and turn in so many different directions at once while bouncing and rolling across the pavement without letting go of the handlebars. I wished I had my mom's Polaroid with me!

All we saw moving down the street, in a pile that was Roger and his bike, was the slow spinning of his front tire. We ran down the street to get to him. He was still not moving. We were in front of the grumpy, old, nasty neighbor's house. He came running out fast. We were gonna run, but we couldn't leave Roger.

The man ran right by us and picked the bike off of Roger. He said in a concerned, loud voice, "You OK, boy?"

Nothing.

He picked Roger up off the street and placed him gently on his lawn.

"You oughta get his mother," he said.

We froze.

"Now!" he shouted.

Peter, Micky, and Keith ran to Roger's house as fast their PF Flyers could take them. I stayed with Roger.

"I'm Mark. What's his name, boy?"

"Roger," I answered. "Is he all right?"

"Roger, can you hear me?" Mark said. "Roger ... Roger!" he repeated.

No response.

"Hmmmm" was all that Mark could muster up while shaking his head. I started to get lightheaded.

"Sit down before you fall down, boy!" Mark said to me. "What's your name?"

"Joey," I mumbled.

"We'll get through this, Joey," Mark assured me.

Just then Roger started to groan and move slowly. When he opened his eyes and saw Mark leaning over him, he bolted upright and screamed, "Don't hurt me!"

"Take it easy, Roger," Mark said.

"How do you know my name?" Roger said in a terrified voice. He looked and saw me sitting next to him and calmed down a little.

"What happened?" Roger asked.

"You fell off your bike," Mark said with a smile. "You had us worried."

This was the first time I had ever seen him smile. *Is this really the grumpy, old man?* I thought.

"You OK, Roger?" I asked.

Roger nodded slightly.

"Can you stand up, boy?" Mark asked.

Roger gave another slight nod as he slowly tried to stand. He fell back down and grabbed his ankle. Just then we started to hear running sneakers getting closer. It was Peter, Micky, and Keith with Roger's mom a few steps behind.

"You Roger's mom?" Mark asked.

"Yes. What happened? Is he all right? Roger, are you all right?" his mom asked in a concerned voice.

Roger sort of nodded yes.

"He just fell off his bike. He seems all right, but he bumped his head and may have hurt his ankle," Mark said.

Roger got up slowly but couldn't stand on his own, so Mark helped carry him home.

When we all got there, Mark sat Roger down on the front porch bench. "You OK now, boy?" Mark asked.

Roger nodded with a slight smile on his face.

"All right then. Take good care of that boy," Mark said with a smile. He then started to walk back home."

"Thank you for looking out for Roger!" his mom shouted.

The rest of us yelled, "Thanks, Mark!"

Without turning back, Mark waved. Things would be different between Mark and us, I thought. *I guess he's not so grumpy after all.*

Roger's mom took him to their doctor's office. A few hours later, she pulled back up the driveway. We followed her car up on our bikes. She got out of the car, went around to the passenger door, and opened it slowly to help Roger get out. He had a huge ace bandage wrapped around his ankle and was clutching onto a pair of crutches. Roger's eyes were looking at the ground while he showed an embarrassed smile. We looked him up and down then burst out laughing.

"You should have seen yourself rolling down the street!" I laughed.

"We thought you were dead!" Keith yelled.

"We thought the old man was gonna drag you down to his dungeon!" Micky said, then he began laughing again.

"When are you gonna be able to ride again?" Peter asked.

"A week or so," Roger said. "I thought the old man was gonna kill me for riding in front of his house."

We all busted out laughing again. Then we were silent.

"Ya' know, you were pretty lucky Mark was there," I said.

We all looked at each other and nodded.

"He's not so bad, I guess," we all agreed.

Things would be different on our block from then on. For the better.

I don't think I'll ever forget how we judged Mark without really knowing him. It made me think.

CHAPTER 25

Parent Meetings All Day!

July 17

It was another rainy Monday summer morning as I headed out to the office. My first stop was at the local Dunkin' for a breakfast sandwich and coffee. I was definitely not awake before the coffee took hold, so I prayed I wouldn't run into anyone I knew.

I made it back to my car unscathed. The rest of the way to the office, I mentally reviewed the day's calendar. Parent meetings. All day.

Ms. Frenzy had scheduled back-to-back meetings with individual parents who wanted to voice their "concerns" on how the school can be a better place for their offspring.

Around 8:30 a.m., I walked into the main office and greeted the few staff members and parents who were already there then checked in with Ms. Frenzy for an updated list of today's parent meetings. She had scheduled five beginning at 9:00 a.m. I could see that my first two appointments had arrived early.

"Welcome, Monday morning! It's going to be a great day!" I said to myself.

As I sat behind my desk, I fired up the laptop and went through emails while periodically glancing at the early parents staring through my office window. I equivocated this to my dogs staring at me making a cheese sandwich.

Just before the top of the hour, I asked Ms. Frenzy to invite the first parent, Mrs. Selmer, in.

Mrs. Selmer had had three of her daughters already graduate from our esteemed establishment. They were excellent students, each graduating within the top ten of their class. Her fourth daughter would be a senior this year. Let's just say she was not as academically gifted as the others. Not even close. Mrs. Selmer's last daughter, Madison, would be entering freshman year in September. She was here today to ensure Madison would be valedictorian of her class senior year, no matter what it took.

"Thank you for seeing me, Dr. Strat," she began. "My Madison is a talented, hardworking, and outstanding student. I will stop at nothing to see that she gets the absolute best from her four years of high school. Your job is to see that she receives any and all modifications to her schedules that will make her valedictorian senior year. My husband and I are adamant about this."

"How does Madison feel about this?" I asked.

"Once I explain it to her, she will be all right with it!" she answered in a lower voice. "As you may or may not know, my husband is an attorney and we will fight every grade injustice throughout Madison's time here."

"Mrs. Selmer, every student in this high school is offered the opportunity to succeed over their four years. I'm certain that Madison will accept each opportunity and do the absolute best she can," I said.

"Not good enough!" Mrs. Selmer countered. "You will see to it that she does. She *will* be valedictorian!

"Let's keep in touch, Mrs. Selmer. Our teachers are more than happy to communicate with you on Madison's progress. Having involved parents like you certainly shapes how your child progresses."

She looked in my direction, taken a little off guard, then lifted her chin high enough where her face could look down on me. "Thank you for your time. I'm sure we understand each other," she said while exiting the office in an Oscar-worthy performance.

I took two Advil prior to my 9:30 a.m. meeting.

Both Mr. and Mrs. Gray entered my office with the last three student yearbooks in tow.

Before I could formally greet them, they sat down and said, "We want Mr. Hall fired! He's a lousy yearbook advisor. Just look at this!" they said as they opened marked pages in all three yearbooks.

"What exactly am I looking at?" I said while thinking about where I might go for lunch today.

"Can't you see?" they said while pointing at several pages. "Our son, Dorian, is in fewer pictures than everyone else in his class. And he's always in the background. On this group shot, his name isn't even listed. This is "bu&s@$!" they said. *"Why does Mr. Hall hate our son?"*

My mind briefly drifted to the long line of staff members just waiting to take over as yearbook advisor. Oh wait … No one wanted this thankless job!

"Mr. and Mrs. Gray, I'm confident this is not intentional. Let me check into this when the staff returns. This is—" I was cut off.

"We want him fired! We're going to the superintendent! He's being singled out! Bullied! Harassed! You'll see. You'll be sorry!" they shouted as they gathered their yearbooks and left in a huff.

Just one more Advil before the next meeting, I thought.

Ms. Frenzy guided in my next appointment with Mrs. Bach, who was president of the band parents association. Her son, Maynard, had been the first chair trumpet player in the concert band, marching band, and orchestra since freshman year. He would be a senior in September.

"Can I level with you, Dr. Strat?" she began with a smile and a wink. "We both know Maynard has been a major asset to our instrumental program for the past three years. Music is in his blood. He eats, drinks, and sleeps brass. You could say he's a 'horny' kid ... Sorry, music joke. Well, I just had my third conversation with Mrs. Keller about getting him the full scholarship he deserves to the Juilliard Conservatory in the city. Can you believe, after being first trumpet for three years and entering his fourth, she says he should apply but he should also explore other options? Other options? He's a natural. Tell me he's not. Does she even know how good he is? I mean, hey, what's the deal?"

At this point, I was trying to assemble my vocabulary in a positive, proactive, and supportive way while trying to get across the sometimes unpleasant facts.

In any high school, especially a group 1 school, just because you were a first chair musician, or quarterback, cheer captain, etc., didn't necessarily mean you were good but that you were the best we had. There it was. How did you say this to a proud parent or to the students themselves? To compound the issue, when it came to performance, even if you graduated from a prestigious institution, it didn't ensure that when you auditioned for a part or role that someone without a degree wouldn't blow you out of the water. How do you prepare the students *and* the parents for the real world—*without getting sued?*

We agreed to work together to explore every possible option for Maynard.

"I'll be standing on the fifty-yard line during the first halftime show cheering him on!" I said as she left, semisatisfied.

"Another Advil wouldn't hurt, would it?" I whispered to myself out loud.

My next meeting was with a middle-aged gentleman I would place in his early forties. He looked familiar but didn't at the same time. He had recently moved into town and was here to register his twin daughters as freshmen.

He looked me in the eyes with a pleasant smile and said in a calm friendly voice, "How are you, Mr. Strat?"

I thought, *Maybe the Advil is finally kicking in! Wait. Mr. Strat?*

"You don't remember me, do you?" he said.

Wait! That voice, smile, eyes, a little less hair ... "Michael! Michael Saxton! It's you!" I said with a beaming smile.

"I knew you wouldn't forget me!" Michael beamed back.

We both got up and gave each other a bro hug.

"You look great! What have you been up to, Michael?" I said. "By the way, would you like a cup of coffee?"

"Sure. Thanks!" he said.

"I just moved back to town. I started three small companies over the past so many years, so I've lived all over. But I'm glad to be back in the area," he said.

"That's wonderful!" I replied. "And you have twin daughters!"

"Yes! Cindy and Sandy. I'm glad they're going to my old alma mater. My wife and I bought a house on Elmwood Ave. We actually met years ago as amateur bird-watchers. We've been together ever since," he said.

"Bird-watching? I never would've guessed. Maybe a rock star, but ... Ya' never know!" I joked.

"You probably don't know this, Mr. Strat, but you were one of my favorite teachers. I was quiet and always sat in the back of the classroom. I was actually going to quit school. It really wasn't for me. Give me a guitar and a cigarette and I was happy! But I liked going to your class because you were a little crazy. I never knew what you were going to do next. Well, I stayed. And here I am. A happily married businessman with two wonderful daughters!" he said in a nostalgic voice. "Thank you!"

As you can imagine, my day, my week, my month, and even my year were complete. I guess we did make a difference, and we didn't even know it. Was I accomplishing my goal of making a difference? Had I already accomplished it? Was there more to come?

I was glad my last meeting was canceled.

I went through the rest of the day with a smile on my face that no one understood. For the first time since summer began, I had a good night's sleep.

CHAPTER 26

Goose!

July 20, 1964

"Joey … Joey … Wake up!" my brother TJ whispered while rocking my shoulder. "We're goin' fishing! Come on!"

I could see my kid brother, Bud, standing behind him with a big grin on his face and nodding in excitement with his plastic fishing pole in hand.

"Come on! It rained last night. I got a ton of night crawlers off the driveway. We're all set. Come on!" TJ insisted.

I looked over at the clock on my nightstand. The big hand was on the four, covering the small hand on the same number. It was pitch-black outside. Before I could say anything, my brothers rolled me out of bed and onto the floor.

"Pile on!" Bud said as they both jumped on me.

"Well, now that I'm up, let's go fishing!" I said, still half asleep.

TJ already had our poles leaning against the bikes on the side of the house. He grabbed a few hooks and bobbers from Dad's tackle box along with a couple of slices of bread as backup bait.

The sand pit we fished at was right behind the lake only a short trip by bike. It was still dark as we left on the day's adventure.

When we arrived at the side street to go onto the path to our secret fishing spot, Bud pulled out his Cub Scout flashlight that glowed but didn't really do the job. He rolled his eyes and shoved it back in his pocket. We managed to get to our special spot when our eyes finally became more adjusted to the darkness. We were the only ones there, and that made it special.

We jabbed the worms, wrapped them, then jabbed them again onto our hooks. TJ snapped bobbers on our lines, and we threw out our first cast. The first cast was always the most exciting. Then we waited.

As sunlight began to show over the far end of the sand pit, we sat silently looking out at our bobbers. We didn't need to talk. It was just nice to be there. Other than a few mild tugs at Bud's line, the water was pretty still.

Now the sun was coming up faster, reflecting off the water. The chill of the early morning air was gone. It was going to be a hot one.

Bud pushed me and said, "Look! Ducks! Coming on the sand over by the lake!"

"They're geese," TJ said while rolling his eyes. "Geese!"

"What's the difference? Let's go look. There are twelve of 'em. And a few babies. I wanna get a baby!" Bud shouted.

"Let's just look, OK?" I said while grabbing at Bud's shirt.

We pulled our lines in then started the short walk to where the geese were coming ashore. We walked slower as we got closer. They seemed not to notice us at first. But all at once, the geese stopped and looked in our direction. We stopped, too!

Then Bud ran toward the geese shouting, "I want one!"

We started to chase him but stopped short as Bud kept running and laughing toward the geese. The geese huddled up then set up like NFL players.

"Oh sh@*!" TJ said under his breath. "Get out of there, Bud!" he shouted.

Bud, just now realizing what was happening, pivoted and ran screaming back in our direction. We did the same.

We looked back and saw the attacking geese slowing down then finally stopping. We stopped too, looked at each other, then started cracking up with laughter. Maybe just a little too early. Apparently one goose, the biggest, of course, started running toward Bud again. TJ saw it. I saw it ... Bud didn't see it.

We pointed for Bud to turn around as we shouted, "Goose! Goose!"

Bud turned around, saw what was happening, and started to run in all directions yelling, "Goose! Goose! Gooooosse!"

He didn't know where else to run so he jumped into the sand pit trying to stay under water where the goose couldn't get him. The goose flapped its wings over the water, for what seemed like an eternity, then went away to join the others.

TJ and I began laughing again, even harder. Every time Bud popped his head out of the water, we pointed behind him yelling, "Goose! Goose! Goose!"

Finally TJ and I jumped in the water with Bud, and we all started laughing and dunking each other under. The water felt good as the sun grew hotter.

After a while, we went back to fishing as the morning sun quickly dried out our clothes. Every now and then in the dead silence, one of us would turn to Bud and yell, "Goose!" at the top of our lungs. Even Bud got into the act.

"I think Bud likes his new name," I said to TJ.

"Goose it is!" TJ said.

"Goose it is!" I said.

Bud shrugged with a grin. "Goose it is!"

We spent the rest of the day fishing, swimming, and just messing around.

When we finally got home, we were tired, and our tans were a shade darker. We walked through the kitchen door like we just got back from the battlefield. My mother and Dexie looked at the three of us while shaking their heads.

"Where have you been all day?" my mother asked.

As we walked toward the living room, TJ said, "Ask Goose!"

I said, "Ask Goose!"

Bud said, "We went fishing!"

While we headed to our bedrooms to get changed, I could hear Dexie and my mother saying to each other in unison, "Goose?"

CHAPTER 27

Duty Assignments!

July 25

It was once again time for our weekly 10:00 a.m. meeting. But first, coffee and bagels.

"Team," I began, "it's that time of the summer again. We need to schedule room assignments, parking assignments, preps, hall duty, lunch duty, ya' know ... Hell week!"

Mrs. Keller had pretty much checked out at this point. She smiled and said, trying to be serious, "I'm working on it."

Everyone laughed.

"Seriously," I said. "What have we got so far?"

Randomly the team started firing out comments.

- "Mr. Marlboro needs air-conditioning all day, due to his asthma. At least that's what his doctor's note says."
- "Mrs. Otis will need the elevator for the first two months of school. She's having both knees replaced in August."
- "Mr. Methuselah insists on the closest parking spot since he has seniority over everyone ... in the state."
- "Ms. Jitters had a nervous breakdown during cafeteria duty at the end of the school year. She'll be coming back

in September after a summer of bed rest ... and pills ... lots of pills."

- "All of our in-house coaches must have last period prep!"
- "The special ed department wants a common lunch period to ... prep?"
- "It's a good idea not to have Mr. Peeper on hall duty by the girl's locker room entrance."
- "The band director insists he spends the entire day in the band room, or the program will fall apart."
- "Ms. Earnest will do any assignments she's needed for ... She doesn't have tenure yet."
- "Mr. Azul wants only his friends in lunch period 4. Ms. Roho wants only her friends in lunch period 5. It's kind of a political thing."
- "Mrs. Hardass is the union president. Her contract says she can make her own schedule and do whatever she wants."
- "Whatever we schedule Mr. Cross for, he'll think it's unfair and that we're picking on him. He's already emailed us to send him this year's grievance forms."
- "The entire social studies department wants last period off so they can get to their out-of-district coaching duties."
- "The entire science department wants to stay in their labs all day so their projects don't blow up."
- "The mathematics department wants to decide on their own duties since they feel they are the most important."
- "The guidance department wants their duties in the SAC room so they can hold individual and group meetings with their students. And they need a new TV, stereo system, and an open account for gaming apps."

I stared at the team and asked, "Anything else?"

Ms. Frenzy added, "I just received word from the board office that Ms. Digits, our AP calculus teacher, resigned.

"Coffee, anyone?" I asked while shaking my head.

Ms. Cattlevic said, while partially raising her hand, "It sounds like a challenge. Can I give it a go?"

You could hear a pin drop.

I answered, "It is quite a challenge, but—"

Before I could finish my sentence, Mrs. Keller said, "Here ya' go!" and dropped all of her scheduling folders on the table in front of Ms. Cattlevic. "I'll be here to ... help ... if you need any ... ya' know ... suggestions."

"Mrs. Keller," I started. "You can't—"

"It's all right, Dr. Strat. I'll give it a go!" Ms. Cattlevic assured me.

Staring Mrs. Keller down, I said, "That's very kind of you, Ms. Cattlevic. Take a look at it and let me and Mrs. Keller know what you suggest. Mrs. Keller will still proceed with the 'entire' scheduling process. Right, Mrs. Keller?"

"Oh yeah, absolutely!" she said in a less than enthusiastic tone. "Absolutely!"

"Next item." I continued. "Several staff members have been calling. They want to start coming in to get a head start on decorating their rooms. Mrs. Keller and Ms. Cattlevic will meet with Iggy once they figure out where the teachers' room assignments are and when he'll be finished stripping and finishing each hallway. Don't let him tell you they can't walk on the floors until the first day the staff comes in. Also, Coach Slick, tell your coaches to keep the athletes out of the hallways. Iggy and his guys are going nuts! Coffee, anyone? I'm gonna have another cup. Anyone?"

No takers. Maybe I should consider decaf. Nah!

"Next. The maintenance department will be painting the lines on the parking lot for the next two days. You know how *quickly* they work, so everyone parks on the street until Monday. That includes buses. And keep the band off the lots!"

"Next. Why are all the deliveries stacked up in the faculty lounge this year? I thought we were using the cafeteria again," I said.

"Marching band is using it for sectional rehearsals in the morning. Cheerleaders in the afternoon. That reminds me. We need to replace a few ceiling tiles in there. Cheerleaders ..." Coach Slick said, shaking his head and grinning.

"Next. The business administrator is hounding me every day to keep all the doors closed and locked. I know. I know. Just make it happen! And tell the parent booster groups to stop propping the doors open! Coach, tell Mr. Butch, the new football parent president, that we appreciate his enthusiasm, but he can't watch the team shower after every practice! Make that a priority! Also, tell your quarterback to stop aiming for the sousaphone while the marching band performs on the practice field. It's a lawsuit waiting to happen. And stop high-fiving him when he does!"

"Next. I've contacted Captain Pike. Several seniors have been stacking up the new picnic tables in the courtyard on the weekends to climb on the roof to party. We'd know who they are if the outdoor cameras worked. Also, we're looking for the culprits who keep painting Mr. Methuselah's parking spot to look like a coffin."

"And Coach, please remind Duke, in a nice way, that he graduated six years ago and doesn't have to show up for football practice every day wearing his varsity jacket. Kinda creepy!"

"OK! Anything else for the good of the order?" I asked.

Mrs. Keller said, "I'll be on vacation next week."

Coach Slick said, "Me too!"

Mr. Bland said, Me too!"

Ms. Sharp said, "Me too!"

Ms. Frenzy said, "Me too!"

"Who scheduled this? Who approved it?" I asked, very confused.

"I guess I did," Ms. Frenzy said. "There were so many papers to go through when I took over for Mrs. Lass. I thought you already approved them ... Sorry."

"Can anyone change their week?" I asked.

All eyes stared at the floor.

"Come on guys, anyone?" I asked again.

Silence.

Once again, I'm f@&#%$! and too nice a guy to direct them to change.

"OK, OK. Looks like it's just you, me, and Iggy, Ms. Cattlevic," I said.

"We got this, Dr. S!" she said with a thumbs up. "We got this."

I smiled as my mind drifted off to the retirement PD I had scheduled for this afternoon with the State Principals Association. Summer was half over. Where did the time go?

CHAPTER 28

Dexie

July 22, 1964

I didn't see a lot of my sister, Dexie. Oh sure, dinnertime, watching cartoons, and in the kitchen. But when she was not hanging out with Mom, she was in her room or out with her four best friends. They'd been together since kindergarten and in every class since then. Brownies, Girl Scouts, cheerleading, softball … Always together. Since they all lived within three blocks from each other, they alternated playing at each other's house. When they were meeting at our house, I was usually leaving as they were arriving.

Today was "cootie" day at my house. Fortunately, it was a slightly cloudy and cool day. Perfect for not being home. Unfortunately, Roger wasn't able to ride his scraped-up Schwinn due to the wheelie incident. The best he could do was hop around his yard since he hated using his crutches. We tried taking turns riding him around on our monkey bars, but his mom put a real fast stop to that. So today we gathered at his house directly across the street from mine.

We were sitting on his front porch trading baseball cards and chewing the stale gum sticks that came in the five-card pack when we saw my sister and her friends come out to the front yard. They began doing somersaults and handstands and attempted splits. It was embarrassing to watch. Like a train wreck. But we couldn't look away. We could make fun, though.

"Look at me! I'm Dexie!" I mocked as I did a lame cartwheel.

My friends laughed. The girls ignored.

Roger yelled loud enough for the girls to hear, "I could do better on my crutches!"

We laughed again. And again, the girls ignored.

Dexie did a back handspring, and yeah, it was good. But to stay in character, we mocked. Micky tried it and landed flat on his back, knocking all the air out of him—and then some.

"I'm all right!" he hissed in a distressed voice. He lay there strong. We knew he was out for the count.

"But can you do a backflip?" we shouted across the street.

Dexie looked at us briefly with a deadpan face then did three back handsprings in a row and ended with a back flip. Perfect landing.

We briefly froze in amazement.

"We can do that!" Peter shouted. "Watch!"

Oh, the embarrassment as we tried to do some moves while maintaining any modicum of dignity. The girls laughed but didn't mock. They upped the ante by building a pyramid with Dexie at the top. They posed and then Dexie, with a grin, did a flip off the top. The girls caught her as she added a spin. It was hard to maintain character with our mouths gaped open so we pretended to ignore them. After all, we showed those … Girls! Our reward was to get some snacks at the corner deli. The girls followed a few minutes later. Must be some sort of psych-us-out game.

"We were here first, cootie carriers! You could follow us afterward, but do not forget to bow first!" Keith said.

We were amused. They were not!

A group of high school boys on bikes stopped in the deli lot.

They began to chum up to my sister and her friends. We objected. They were much too old ... High school!

I said to my sister, "Come on. Let's head back."

The older boys laughed and pushed by me, making us seem like idiots.

"All right, girls! What do say we become, ya' know, more familiar with each other?" one of the boys said.

The others walked by pushing me and Keith to the ground. I got up ready to fight but hoping not too. Keith pushed back and got knocked to the ground, again.

They approached the girls saying, "You're coming with us. It'll be fun. You little boys, stay."

That was it. "You talkin' to me?" I said.

They looked and laughed as they headed closer to my sister. This wasn't going to end well.

"Stay away from my sister!" I said in an authoritative voice. It was at that point he pushed me down again. My team got up ready for anything. The oldest boy put his arm around my sister.

I yelled, "Get 'em!" as we attacked ... and failed.

Dexie was surprisingly calm. She turned to him with a sweet smile on her face then kneed him in the gems. When he doubled over, she popped him in the jaw just to straighten him back up. Her other friends had the rest of the boys under control like they were swatting gnats away on a summer night.

"That's my brother and his friends. You fu$@ with them again, we'll be back. Got it? ... Got It!" Dexie said in a firm but aggressive low voice.

Then she punched him in the eye. "Only I can make fun of my brother and his friends. *Got it?*"

The boys hopped on their bikes like they were being chased by leopards. Within seconds, they were out of sight. We looked at my sister and her friends. There was nothing said, but the silence spoke volumes … Family is family! And sometimes friends are family. Wouldn't have it any other way.

We walked together back to our house as if nothing had ever happened.

CHAPTER 29

Just the Two of Us

July 31

It was Monday morning, once again, at the very end of July. It was going to be an interesting week with the majority of the summer staff on vacation.

As I pulled into the school parking lot, everything went fuzzy. Was it the caffeine? Anxiety? *Stroke?* Nope ... Nope ... None of the above. It seemed our crackerjack maintenance crew delayed painting the parking lot lines until late Friday afternoon—as the rain began. The storm continued for a good twelve hours! So on this very bright sunny Monday morning, what I saw could best be described as the result of a thousand birds releasing their bomb bay doors all over the lot. It was so bad that the band didn't know where to line up ... *I know, right?*

I parked where I believed was my spot, and as I got out of the car, I could see Iggy and a few of his crew taking selfies and using the parking lot as a backdrop. Quite creative poses, too!

I shook my head and entered the building through the boiler room door because it was closer and propped open. Why would it be locked?

I arrived at the main office just as Ms. Cattlevic was coming in the front entrance. This door was also propped open.

"Good morning, Reagan," I said.

"Good morning, Joe," she answered.

We stopped, turned our heads toward each other, and laughed. This was the first time either of us had addressed each other by our first names.

"It's going to be a long week," I said.

Reagan nodded as we walked behind the counter on the way to our offices.

"Let's meet around 9:30-ish to go over this week's schedule," I said.

Ms. Cattlevic gave a thumbs up.

I tried not to open work emails yesterday, so this morning I was greeted with ninety-six unread messages. Most of them from neighbors wondering what happened to the parking lot. Others wondered why the courtyard picnic tables were stacked up to the roof.

Nine thirty rolled around as Ms. Cattlevic and I sat down with cups of coffee in the conference room.

I began. "Let's get started."

Immediately, the fire alarm sounded.

"Sh@$!" I shouted. "Come on. I'll show you where the panel is."

Iggy was already there looking at it. "Cafeteria!" he said.

We headed down and realized it was the fire sensor triggered by the heat and dust. The three of us made sure all the students and coaches were out of the building.

Police cars, emergency vehicles, and fire trucks filled the parking lot within minutes. Most of the first responders were former graduates.

The fire chief entered the building and made short work of confirming the problem. It was the sensor in the cafeteria. Iggy reset the alarms and we waved everyone back into the building.

As I turned to thank the crews for coming out so fast, all I could see was a sea of iPhones taking pictures of the parking lot and people posing their best for social media.

When I finally got to the chief and responders to properly thank them, the superintendent popped up with her iPhone aiming our way as she said, "Smile, Joe!" She followed up with "This is for my 10:30 a.m. meeting with our 'current' maintenance department."

"Come on, kid. Let's head back in," I said to Reagan. "Hey, no offense. I have a habit of calling people kid. I don't mean anything by it."

"Not a problem, boss. I'm good with it!" She smiled.

We began our meeting again, starting with class sizes, textbooks, laptops, and supplies. Ms. Cattlevic had studied our scheduling program last week and incorporated a few tweaks of her own. This seemed to address some of the singletons with their individual variables. Apparently Mr. Jopps, our director of technology, guided her through the basics, then she guided him through the modifications needed for this specific schedule.

Some people are natural schedulers. Others work overtime to maintain a dismal second. I am the latter.

Reagan started, "I began looking over the master schedule this weekend. I think we can address many of the issues if we ..."

There was more scheduling chatter.

I studied the screen as Reagan clacked away at the laptop. She not only began looking at the schedule, but she had also easily placed 850 pieces of this thousand-piece puzzle together. I nodded like I knew what she was talking about.

Just to appear relevant, I interjected. "So what you're suggesting is ..." And I added, "Are you certain that will ..."

"And if you insert the duties, preps, and lunch assignments ..." she continued.

I thought, *If I get up to go play on the swing set outside, it might slightly diminish my position of authority.* But that was where I felt I belonged at this moment in time.

"I like the direction you're taking this in. Run with it! It's always good to have a fresh pair of eyes look things over," I said, knowing it was an understatement.

I left her to the scheduling while I read through resumes in my office for our ever-expanding list of vacancies.

Reagan worked through lunch with only a cup of coffee and PB&J sandwich in between elective requests and grade level entries. I had a protein bar for lunch and a walk around the campus to check up on our summer sports and activities. It was a beautiful day to be outside.

"Why am I not on the beach?" I asked myself, with a sigh.

Throughout the afternoon, I focused on calendaring concerts, club activities, etc. around sport schedules, band competitions, the whole nine yards!

When prioritizing the athletic and activities calendar, there are two approaches.

The first is the educational and logical way.

The second is the politically astute way.

I will now analyze my options.

Out of our nine current board members, two have kids on the football team, one on the competition cheerleading squad, two with kids in the band, and one with the trifecta.

Of the remaining three seats, one has been on the board for twenty-seven years mainly to be the voice of unreason. One aspires to working their way up to mayor, and the last has advanced degrees in education. She is usually voted down unless supporting arts or athletic issues.

Our superintendent, Harriet Fieldman, is also coming to the end of her five-year contract, and Jupiter is aligning with Mars.

Oh, and there will be three open board seats this year. Three of the four potential candidates are girls softball parents. The fourth has three children in the charter schools.

Under normal circumstances, Mr. Minor, Coach Slick, and Mrs. Keller would develop the calendar with the input of the club advisors, coaches, and staff. But since Ms. Cattlevic was amusing herself with what appeared to be the "light work" of scheduling the building, I decided to attack the calendar with the available data.

"Who to appease? Who to appease?" I pondered. "I guess I could ask all the parent group presidents. The last one standing wins, kinda like a game show.

Now that's a fundraiser! I thought. *It beats duct-taping the principal to the cafeteria wall.*

"Ah yeah," I said out loud. "Can't forget the middle and elementary schools when calendaring concerts, graduation ceremonies, and the like, so parents don't have to decide who is going to which event."

After a long afternoon, it was time to go home. I could finish this tonight on my deck with a bourbon, straight up.

Reagan and I locked up and headed home.

After dinner I went out to the deck with my folders and some bourbon … The mosquitoes were biting. I hated mosquitoes!

CHAPTER 30

Safe Summer Fun!

July 28, 1964

"I love mosquitoes!" I shouted as the entire neighborhood followed the mosquito fogging trucks on their bikes.

The idea was to inhale the fog and blow it out like we were smoking. Very cool! We chased it for blocks. More kids from other neighborhoods joined in until the truck finally stopped at the huge town garage behind the municipal building. We circled around the parking lots then headed back to our neighborhoods in groups. The afternoon would bring more entertainment as our block was scheduled to be repaved.

As early afternoon arrived, trucks gathered at the end of our block for the street paving ritual. We sat on my front lawn to enjoy the show!

The paving process happened every three years or so. A truck would go up the block on one side and down the other spraying tar. A half hour later, another truck would do the same, dropping loose gravel. It was during that half hour that the fun began. We would gather sticks and leaves to scoop up the tar and spread it on various objects around the yard. Very sticky. Micky and Keith, on the other hand, were happy just rolling stones into the tar. This seemed to give them some kind of satisfaction.

Ultimately, one of the little kids would try to walk across it. When it was too late to realize what they were doing, they had the distinct honor of wearing the tar on their feet for the remainder of the summer. Their parents would try anything to get it off, including pouring gasoline on it to thin it out. The smell of fresh gasoline combined with the mosquito fog was priceless!

Roger's little sister, Jill, made the mistake of trying to cross the street on her Schwinn as the gravel truck was approaching. She tipped over, leaving tar not only on her bike but head to toe on her right side as well. And yes, that included her hair. We were horrified but laughing at the same time. She, of course, was crying uncontrollably. Her mother came running outside to gather her and the bike up while destroying her pink, fuzzy slippers ... Again, priceless!

Later that day, she could be seen sporting a short, cropped, shag haircut. We tried not to laugh, but ... Just then, out walked her twin sister, Carol, with the same haircut in support of Jill.

For the next day or two, we watched traffic driving slowly up and down the block trying not to scratch their cars with the gravel shooting up as it settled. We knew better than to ride our bikes on it.

When the weekend arrived, my father handed out rags and tar remover for me, my brothers, and my sister to get the tar off the rotted metal on the fenders and bumpers of our sky-blue Ford Fairlane.

CHAPTER 31

It's Going to Be a Great Day!

August 1

It was only Tuesday morning as I walked through the main office entrance with two Dunkin's in hand.

"OMG! Thank you!" I cried out loud, looking up at the heavens as tears formed in my eyes. "You're back!"

Sitting behind her desk, with crutches leaning against the filing cabinet, was Mrs. Lass! She was having a conversation with Ms. Cattlevic when she saw me come in.

With a huge smile, she shouted, "Yes, I'm back. But I'm not getting up. Get over here!"

I ran!

"I'm soooo glad to see you! How are you!" I babbled. "I see you've met Reagan."

"Yes, she's wonderful! Did you miss me?" she said, obviously knowing the answer.

"Are you kidding? So much has been going on," I said.

"So I hear. Reagan says you have everything under control," Mrs. Lass said, looking impressed.

I looked at Reagan and said, "I owe you, By the way, I have coffee for both of you!"

"Mrs. Lass made coffee before I got here. It's pretty good. Not that yours isn't," Reagan said as she shared a knowing glance and smile with Mrs. Lass.

"But thank you," they both responded.

For the next half hour, we caught up on Mrs. Lass's health and family. We then segued to our summer "progress" to date.

Mrs. Lass, still smiling, shook her head. "What do we need?"

"Well, it's just the three of us through Friday. Help!" I answered.

Mrs. Lass wasted no time firing up her computer. "Let's go!" she hollered. "Where do we stand on the master schedule?"

Ms. Cattlevic turned her laptop so Mrs. Lass could see.

"Who did this?" Mrs. Lass asked.

"Reagan," I said a little sheepishly.

Mrs. Lass stared directly at me and said, "Wow! How long did this take you, Reagan?"

"Oh about a week or so," Reagan replied.

Again, Mrs. Lass said, "Wow! Wow."

I said, "I thought it would be a good idea for Reagan to continue to work on the schedule while we—"

"Good idea," Mrs. Lass interrupted with a smirk on her face. "I'll run up your old welcome-back letters and parent/student packets. Has anyone worked on the purchase orders?"

"Uh, no?" I whispered.

Again, the stare.

"Locks? Locker assignments?" she asked while squinting in my direction.

I shook my head.

"Textbooks?" she asked with that same stare.

I forced a grin and didn't answer.

"And everyone's on vacation?" she asked, knowing the answer.

I nodded with the same shamed grin on my face.

I'll go play on the swings now, I thought.

"OK, I think I got it. Why don't I get reestablished here

while you get me the list of candidates we need to schedule for interviews?" Mrs. Lass said, already looking exhausted.

I nodded and quickly went to my office to ... do stuff.

Interviewing candidates in early August is like showing up to an all you can eat buffet fifteen minutes before it closes ... Slim pickings. We have our in-house candidates who receive obligatory interviews, out-of-district candidates who are right out of college, and administrative candidates looking for their first administrative position right out of the classroom. The remainder were candidates with way too many years in education and not budget friendly. Then there were the jumpers. Jumpers were interesting. They usually had the longest resumes due to the many districts they'd been in over a very short period of time.

Now add to this process the frustration of waiting sixty days from the candidates board approval date then resignation from their previous district. Unless the previous district released them early ...

Now it was the first week of August. Do the math. And if your new hire bails on their previous district to start the new year with your district, don't be surprised when they do it to you in the future.

Then, of course, once hired, new staff appreciation and loyalty could last a lifetime. But with others, the expiration date was when they blossomed from their neophyte cocoon to a beautifully tenured staff member and future union president.

Very few resumes were coming in. When they did, I immediately searched social media. Then if no major red flags popped up, I would do a brief introductory phone interview.

In the depths of my mind, I was thinking, *Do I settle for someone with a pulse or go the substitute route for September?*

Many times they are one and the same. I guess it's difficult searching for high-quality educators with the school slogan "We are Ave Ridge!"

Mrs. Lass made short work of catching up on what needed to be done. Together, we regained our old rhythm and made lists and agenda items for Monday's meeting when my administrative team returned from vacation.

"It's good to have you back," I said with a sincere smile.

"I know," she said as she smiled. "It's good to be back."

A lot got done over the next few days. Mrs. Lass was great, Mrs. Cattlevic was a wonderful addition to the team, and I ... I was very fortunate.

Four more weeks until Labor Day weekend.

CHAPTER 32

Mastering Wheelies, Part 2! Where's Mark?

August 1, 1964

Roger's ankle was feeling better so he wasn't using his crutches, but he was still limping a little. Strong enough to pull himself up into the tree fort but not strong enough to ride his bike, so we spent the morning climbing the fort and trees just hangin' out.

Noon approached but we skipped lunch and headed to the baseball fields on our bikes instead. I shared my banana seat with Roger, which his mother seemed to be fine with, now that his ankle was a little better. The fields were pretty crowded for a Saturday. A lot of pickup games were going on. We could see Tommy pitching on field one with the older kids. I think he slept there. The rest of the fields were just as busy so we rode behind them where the grass was green and thick.

Peter shouted, *"Wheelie time?"*

We looked at each other, surprised at the mere suggestion. "Let's do it!" we all agreed.

Fortunately, we had been watching the older kids in the upper numbers of the neighborhood and believed we knew where we went wrong the first time.

We leaned our bodies forward over the handlebars as we pedaled evenly. We pulled back as if we were in a rocking chair while still pedaling and shifting to the front of our banana seats. Our arms were outstretched as we kept our balance by sticking out a knee on either side as needed. This was mostly a reflex. And as we found out the hard way, a sissy bar was not your friend! When we fell, and we did fall, we learned to roll. This was so much easier on thick grass than on hard asphalt.

Roger sat on the sidelines applauding and taking mental notes. The rest of us took turns popping wheelies one at a time, critiquing and applauding after each attempt. Our confidence was building, as well as grass stains all over our clothes. These we wore like badges of honor.

Tommy and a couple of the older kids joined us after the baseball games broke up. We started to feel like we were actually going to be middle schoolers. The older kids had a better grasp of the wheelie and offered suggestions as we went along. Eventually, we got the hang of it. The more we tried, the longer we stayed up on the back wheel. A short time later, we were pros … or thought so anyway.

It was getting hotter and hotter as the afternoon went on. Easily above ninety degrees. We needed to get out of the sun and find some shade. Tommy said he was disappointed when everyone left.

Roger hitched a ride back on Micky's bike with Keith, Peter and me leading the way. We landed our bikes on the front lawn of my house and headed to the hose in the back. Micky stopped and let Roger off with a smoother landing then met us at the hose. The water hit the spot. Even the warm water on the first few sips. I have gained an appreciation for the taste of rubber and water on a hot summer day.

We spent the rest of the afternoon sitting under the shade of the trees by the steel shed in my backyard until dinnertime.

One by one my friends headed to their individual homes for dinner.

Once a month on a mid-Sunday morning, Dad would try his hand at making sausage, meatballs, and rigatoni that would feed an army. The first serving was midafternoon. The next three were on alternating days through the week and it was just as good each time. This was one of those days. You couldn't rush through eating, or you could wear it on your shirt for the rest of the night. So it took slightly longer before I would meet my friends back at the end of my driveway.

Even though the sun was beginning to set behind our tree-lined block, it felt like it was still in the eighties. Since Roger couldn't play kickball, he brought along a bright red Wham-O Frisbee. The five of us set up in the middle of the road tossing it in a five-way pattern, standing a comfortable distance from each other, trying not to run too much. This kept us from overheating, and Roger wouldn't have to run or twist his ankle.

Peter gave one last serve to Roger with a little too much height. It landed on the grumpy old man's—I mean Mark's—front lawn. We hadn't really seen Mark around for quite a while.

"Maybe he's on vacation," I said.

"Should we get it?" Keith asked while looking at each of us for some sort of approval.

"I guess so," I said. "It's close to the road."

"You get it!" Micky said, sounding a little nervous but smiling.

We inched our way toward Mark's front yard feeling confident, yet not, at the same time. There was more nervous laughter accompanied by light pushing and shoving.

"There're no lights on inside," Roger said.

"It's not dark out," I mocked.

"Well, here we are," Peter said, stating the obvious.

We stood there on the edge of his property for a good five minutes like we were waiting for a bus.

"Ahh, this is silly," I said. "Come on!"

The second we stepped onto his lawn, Mark slammed open the front door and jumped onto the porch.

"He's got a gun!" Micky screamed at the top of his lungs.

We froze in place, terrified as Mark ran down the steps and toward the Frisbee brandishing not one, but two huge water pistols!

"You want it, come and get it!" he shouted.

We looked at each other then ran toward the Frisbee laughing. Mark hit us with streams of water like a marksman. Every time we got close, we got soaked, yet we came back for more.

When the pistols were finally empty, Mark exclaimed, "Uh oh, out of ammo!" and ran back up the stairs and into his house laughing. "Damn kids!"

We couldn't believe it. We grabbed the Frisbee still laughing in disbelief. We waved to Mark, who was at his front window smiling. He waved back then turned away.

We were soaked, which was just as well. Otherwise, some of us may have had to excuse ourselves to change our shorts … ya' know …

"*What just happened?*" Roger said, still in shock.

"I dunno, but that was crazy!" Peter said while still laughing.

We slowly walked to the corner deli, still laughing and looking back at Mark's house.

We entered the deli, soaking wet, and stood in front of the large fans by the ice cream counter trying to dry off. Each of us made our ice pop selection, paid, then headed back to my driveway.

For the remainder of the night, we just hung out until it was dark. When I went inside, my family was sitting in front of the Zenith watching *My Favorite Martian*, so I joined them then fell asleep on the floor.

August 2, 1964

Sunday morning came fast.

Sundays were very relaxing, especially in the summer. My dad, who normally got up at 5:30 a.m. every morning, slept in on the weekends until around 5:45 a.m. He routinely got into the Fairlane for his morning drive to the deli across town. For whatever reason, he said it was better than the one around the corner. He always came home with the same items: a copy of the *New York Daily News,* the *Newark Star Ledger,* and the local *Record.*

On his way back into the house, he would bring the milk in from the milk box at the foot of the front steps. Once inside, he would take his place at the head of the dining room table and open the *Star Ledger* while lighting his first Kent of the day.

Being Sunday, today's papers were three times the size of the weekly papers and included the bright colors of the funnies wrapped around the outside. Sunday was also the day he stopped at the bakery for a box full of doughnuts. These usually included jelly doughnuts smothered in confectionery sugar, glazed crullers, crumb cake squares, and chocolate doughnuts.

I woke up on the living room floor exactly where I fell asleep. Mom and Dad were already at the dining room table. I crawled my way to the TV to turn on the morning cartoons then flopped onto the couch. A little while later, the others would stumble their way downstairs.

My father was enjoying his second cup of Sanka while my mother was busy making fried bologna and scrambled eggs for the family. She also toasted up something new. Pop-Tarts! This surprise was by far the best part of the breakfast.

We all sat at the table glomming down the hot breakfast, Pop-Tarts, and some doughnuts. We also took the opportunity to use our Silly Putty to copy the colored funnies and stretch the characters into weird expressions.

By the time my mother sat down to join us, we were already finished and watching cartoons in the living room. My father didn't even look up from his crossword puzzle even though some of our plates on the table were still spinning. My mother shook her head with an expressionless look on her face and took her first sip of a steamy cup of tea.

After she finished her breakfast, Mom shouted into the living room, "We're leaving for Grandma and Grandpa's house in an hour. Get dressed! Wear something nice … and clean!"

We cheered! Who doesn't like going to their grandparents' house? But first, we had to see if Elmer Fudd caught the rabbit.

"Get dressed! Now!" my mother shouted again.

We got up slowly. Slow enough to see that Bugs got away again. Then we ran upstairs to get dressed.

A half hour later, my father yelled, "Time to go! Let's go!"

When my father said it was time to go, it was time to go. Right then. No second warning. Trust me.

We filed out of the house and took our usual spots in the station wagon, where my father was cranking all the windows down and the back window flipped up and locked into place. He hopped into the driver's seat, adjusted his mirror, opened the front wing window, then started the car and lit a Kent. We were on our way!

There were no beach chairs or coolers to block the rotted steel over the wheel wells this time so Goose and I made a game out of who can come closest to touching the speeding back tires first. That game and the smell of exhaust always reminded me of the trips to my grandparents' house.

My grandparents lived twenty minutes east toward the city. They'd lived in that area all their life and would never think of moving away.

It was now late morning when Dad pulled the wagon into the long driveway, where we raced out and ran inside.

My grandmother was already in the kitchen, busy making the Sunday dinner, and my grandfather was finishing up some … paperwork.

Grandpa must have loved math because he always had pieces of paper on the coffee table with a lot of numbers and dollar signs, names, and phone numbers all over them when he listened to the horse races on the transistor radio in the den. He would get a lot of phone calls after each race where he talked nothing but numbers. As for my grandma, she worked for years at the candy store across Main Street. Her house was always filled with the best candy a kid could want!

My grandmother was famous for her handmade cheese raviolis. This was always accompanied by a huge serving plate of meatballs, sausage, pork on the bone, and hand-rolled braciola in her homemade sauce: gravy, *sugo,* or whatever. It was great!

She would say to us, "The secret to making raviolis is to roll them out so they're paper-thin. When you get to that point, roll them thinner. If you take the time to continue this process, you'll know exactly when they're finally ready for the ricotta cheese, or pot cheese."

No one ever came close to duplicating them. They just melted in your mouth. The homemade Italian bread always came out just before the main course. You needed this to sop up the sauce, gravy, whatever.

When dinner was ready, we all gathered around the dining room table ready for the feast. My grandfather sat at the head of the table with my dad to his left. Grandma sat at the other end closest to the kitchen. The rest of us sat on both sides of the huge wooden table, already picking at the bread. My parents and grandparents opened up some Ballantine's beer and a jug of port wine. We got soda. Lots of soda.

At the start of the meal was when my grandfather always said to the four of us, "Don't fatten up on the bread and soda! Grandma worked hard on those ravis!"

We were built to eat, and we did not disappoint! Sparks were flying off our silverware as my grandfather looked at us in amazement. My grandmother just smiled and kept the food coming. The four adults chatted and ate, while the four of us just ate.

We finished in record time and sat quietly. Well, what we thought was quietly, while the adults finished their meals.

Next came the desserts. After a few scoops of Neapolitan ice cream, fresh cannoli, and some home-baked chocolate chip cookies, we became restless. We were ready to run around their backyard. This is when my mother helped Grandma clear the table and wash the dishes, and my father and grandpa pulled out a deck of cards.

They had a small backyard, but just enough room to run around, kick a soccer ball, and climb some trees. There were no kids our age around their neighborhood so I was sure the neighbors loved hearing us scream and yell for the next half hour.

Afterward, we followed TJ, who was running back into the house to grab more chocolate cookies and soda. With our fists filled, we jumped on the living room furniture to claim seats, couches, and anything else comfortable to settle in on until it was time to go home.

Dexie turned on the TV, switching the channels back and forth to look for cartoons. I tried adjusting the antenna on top of the set, Reynolds Wrap and all. The only channel that worked had the Yankees game on. My father and grandfather looked over with a smile of approval. Dexie was not as enthusiastic, but we all watched the game anyway.

When the game was over, my mother and grandma finished their coffee, and my father shouted at my grandfather, "You beat me again? That's it! I'm done!" That was when we knew we were getting ready to leave. My father sealed the deal by saying, "It's time to go!"

It always took a long time to say goodbye, hug, kiss, and say goodbye again, before we hopped back into the station wagon and headed home. Grandma and Grandpa were the best.

We listened to music on WABC without saying a word all the way home. We were all comfortable and full.

The sun was just setting as we pulled back into our driveway. We jumped out of the car and headed to the living room just in time for Lassie, followed by *Walt Disney's Wonderful World of Color* on our black-and-white TV.

Mom made two bowls of Jiffy Pop. One for Dad, the other for us. The windows to the house were wide-open with two large fans facing us as we watched TV.

At 9:00 p.m., we brushed our teeth and then went to bed.

CHAPTER 33

The Team Is Back!

August 7

Agenda

- Schedule Update
- Sports & Activities Calendar
- Staff Vacancies
- Room Assignments
- New Staff Orientation
- More Coffee Breaks
- Update My Resume

Please Initial

_____ Dr. Strat, Principal

_____ Ms. Cattlevic, Assistant Principal

_____ Coach Slick, Athletic Director

_____ Mrs. Lass, Executive Administrative Assistant

_____ Director of Guidance, TBD

_____ Guidance Administrative Assistant, TBD

The summer staff arrived between 8:15 and 8:30 a.m. on this cloudy and cool Monday morning. Their first stop was to see Mrs.

Lass, who visibly appreciated the hugs, kisses, and welcome-back shouts. It was a slow start from here so when I announced in a tone more assertive than usual that our meeting would begin promptly at ten o'clock, reality set in.

Ms. Cattlevic, Mrs. Lass, and I went over the agenda in my office prior to the meeting. There were four weeks left before Labor Day weekend and a lot had to be done.

With our best game faces on, we headed to the conference room. I walked behind Mrs. Lass in case she tipped over on those crutches.

Ain't gonna happen on my watch! I thought.

Surprisingly, the team was sitting in their usual spots before 10:00 a.m., not sure what this meeting would bring.

"Let's get started. I hope you all had a good rest last week. It's time to hit the ground running. Keep your laptops closed. No solitaire," I began.

Clicks could be heard around the table of laptops being shut. Their rolling eyes made no sound.

"All right," I said as I handed out a stack of papers. "This is the list of vacancies we have to date. I have done the initial screenings and introductory phone interviews. The interview committee will make time as listed on the handout."

Vacancies

Administrative

- 9:00 a.m. Director of Guidance
- 9:45 a.m. Medical Suite Coordinator/School Nurse

Teachers

- 10:30 a.m. AP Physics Teacher
- 11:15 a.m. AP Calculus Teacher

- 1:00 p.m. HS English Teacher
- 1:45 p.m. Art/Photography Teacher

Office Staff

- 2:30 p.m. Administrative Assistant—Guidance

Maintenance

- All Positions—Superintendent

"Ohhhh, sh*@!" several voices whispered under their breath.

I began reading the list of items that needed to be addressed.

"Coach, I need all the athletic stipend-position job descriptions. They're incomplete and haven't been updated since we offered archery," I said.

Coach responded, "I don't believe I have any—"

Mrs. Lass politely cut him off, saying, "See me."

"*The Student/Parent Handbooks* are complete and ready to go online. Mrs. Keller, Ms. Sharp, and Ms. Frenzy, you'll be in charge of counting and sectioning the authorization and understanding agreement cards by first period home rooms so they'll be ready for distribution the first day of school," I said while scanning the room for body language.

Softly, Mrs. Keller said, "But—"

With a smile on my face, I said, "No buts. Mrs. Keller and Ms. Sharp will begin printing duplicate schedules. Get the mailings ready. Ms. Cattlevic will oversee this."

Mrs. Keller began to interject. "I may be taking a few more days."

In a more direct manner, I said, "Please, Mrs. Keller. We need you here. Iggy, are the rooms ready? I'm letting the teachers in to decorate their classrooms this Friday."

Iggy looked startled, as if his mind were somewhere else. "Well, I'm gonna need a little extra time to—"

Winking at Iggy, I said, "No time left. I know you can do it! Coffee, anyone?"

I looked up from my list and addressed everyone. "We're having our Back to School Night the first full day the teachers are back. The schedules need to go out the Friday before. This way the parents should be in a semigood mood before they know what other students are in their kids' classes and before any grades have been given."

Mrs. Keller asked, "Do we have enough time to—"

Again with a smile, I said, "We'll make it work … Ms. Cattlevic?"

Ms. Cattlevic began. "I've emailed you all a copy of the first day assembly program welcoming the students back, by grade level. There is also a copy of our New Teacher Symposium program for new staff members that will meet once a week on Thursdays for the month of September. All staff members are invited. I've also sent everyone copies of the Back to School Night schedule. We will be having a pizza party for the staff before the parents arrive for the 6:00 p.m. start. Any questions?"

The staff seemed caught off guard. Mrs. Lass, staring at the agenda, had a huge grin on her face as her head nodded up and down.

In a more serious tone, I said, "Iggy, and everyone in this room, the doors must stay closed and locked at all times. Is that clear? I want them checked every half hour. Coach, I'm sure you will relay the importance of this directive to your coaches."

Coach Slick stared at the ground shaking his head and said, "I'll try to get through to them, but—"

Interrupting again, I said, "Not good enough. Make it happen … Mrs. Lass?"

Mrs. Lass addressed the staff. "If anyone needs forms or

permission slips sent home with our mailings, I'll need them by this Friday morning. We will also be sending out student physical forms for doctor confirmation and updated student information cards."

I added, "Nurse Jackie will be splitting her duties between the middle school and high school until another nurse is hired. Iggy, how are your guys progressing with delivering supplies and equipment to the classrooms?"

"We're starting to get the departments," Iggy said in a quieter voice.

I replied in the same volume, "Great! Keep up the good work! ... Ms. Cattlevic?"

All eyes again focused on Ms. Cattlevic. "Staff parking decals and school lanyards are already in their mailboxes. Senior parking decals and all grade level lanyards will be handed out during the extended home room on the first day. Students and staff will have pictures taken for their ID cards during their gym classes the second day back," she said.

Picking up where I left off on the list, I said, "Senior portraits will be taken in three weeks. That's the last Tuesday of this month. Ms. Cattlevic and our senior class advisor will be stationed at the main entrance. Pictures will be taken on the stage. The seniors will use the restrooms at the entrance to get ready. Iggy will make sure they're open and clean. No one goes past the entrance gates! Got it?"

Trying to get my attention, Coach Slick said, "We have a scrimmage that day in—"

I shot a look in his direction.

He thought better of this and said, "I could change it."

"Mr. Jopps, will the network be up and running for the first day?" I asked.

Mr. Jopps began. "Well, the FTP protocol and the hypertext transfer protocol may seem simple but leaves us in a conundrum.

If we, let's say, use the data element on the DSL, then the EDI may change the indicator of the ISDN. So the offsite storage may compromise the peripheral equipment and generate an alternate system function. Then—"

"In English, Mr. Jopps!" I said, in an almost pleading manner.

"Yeah, we should be all set," he replied.

Relieved, I said, "Thank you, Mr. Jopps! I need more coffee, anyone else?"

Mrs. Keller asked in general, "How did the curriculum committee do this summer with the updates?"

Without lifting my head, I responded, "The curriculum committee did an excellent job of doing very little again this year. The board will approve the curriculum at their next meeting."

Everyone nodded as if this was expected.

In conclusion, I said, "By the way, we'll be having a luncheon at the superintendent's office this Friday at twelve noon with the district administrators. You're all expected to be there. With the strict budget requirements sent down by the state, I would eat before you get there."

"Anything else for the good of the order?" I asked, glancing around the table.

"Can we open our laptops now?" Coach Slick whispered in a sardonic tone.

"Knock yourself out," I said. "Meeting's over!"

CHAPTER 34

Camping with My Cousins

August 1–2, 1964

Every August, my dad and his brothers, Hank and Foster, planned a weekend camping trip to the Pocono Mountains. My aunts, Anne and Marie, as well as my mom were definitely not campers, but they came for the family time anyway. I couldn't wait to see all my cousins again. They were all older than us, but we got along and fought like brothers and sisters.

Aunt Marie and Uncle Foster had two boys in college. My cousin Don was their oldest, and Cousin Kevin was two years younger. They were both home from college for the summer.

Uncle Hank and Aunt Anne had Hank Jr., who was in college, and Shanda, who would be a high school senior in September. I had a much older cousin, Chrissie, but she moved to South Dakota so we didn't see a lot of her.

Early Saturday morning, three station wagons lined up in front of our house at the crack of dawn. My dad and uncles shared a thermos of coffee as they double-checked that all of the camping equipment was secured on the roofs of the cars, on the floors, in between us on the seats, and anywhere else there was extra storage.

When Dad gave the high sign, Mom and our aunts loaded us into the cars trying to remember if we had packed everything while also trying to stay awake.

Naturally, we were the lead car, so with black smoke billowing out of the exhausts of all three wagons, we were on our way.

Goose and I were sandwiched between sleeping bags, blankets, and coolers. Dad lifted and locked the back window before we left the house so we could actually breathe and move some of our arms and legs. We waved to our cousins behind us most of the way to the campsite, which my aunt and uncle grew tired of almost immediately.

A little over an hour into the trip, we arrived in the Poconos! Ten minutes later, we turned off the main road and drove across a few half-paved, bumpy roads. The next turn was onto a dusty, dirt road with plenty of potholes. One more half-flooded path, and we were there.

Dexie had only puked twice on this trip. But judging by the drippy paper bags being brought out of the other two cars, the cousins may have beaten our record. Even Aunt Marie looked a little queasy.

We all piled out of the cars ready to help carry the supplies to the campsites. My mom and aunts followed up with a deeper cleaning of the vinyl back seats that made my aunt Marie look even queasier.

In front of us were the usual three cabins on the riverbank. All three had electricity and a common hose for water. Across the path and a bit down the slope were several outhouses with crescent moon cutouts and all. Each cabin was identical inside. One huge room with a divider and four bunk beds, an eating area with a window overlooking the river, and a kitchen area with a small refrigerator, a hot plate, and storage cabinets. Outside we each had a charcoal grill, a firepit, picnic table, and four Adirondack chairs.

The moms immediately began setting up the cabins both

inside and out, while the dads set up the outdoor equipment and gathered wood for the firepits.

My cousins and I ran down to the river to check out the site for fishing and to catch some crayfish. Well, my older cousins actually came along to keep an eye on us, so we'd stay together.

TJ had already tied a rag around his head and sharpened a long stick to spear some fish. He loved this stuff. I was a little more … cautious and liked to observe things until I knew that they were safe. Goose, not so much. He started walking knee high into the river to snag some crayfish when he fell from an underwater ridge on the riverbed floor. He knew how to swim but began to panic and was swept a little downstream. Before anyone else even knew what was happening, TJ dropped his spear, waded through the water, then swam to get Goose. Goose saw him coming and began to calm down a little, but he was still nervously wading. When TJ got there, Goose reached out and climbed on his back. TJ slowly waded back to the river's edge where Dexie was waiting to help him back onto the bank. The older cousins, just now realizing what had happened, looked at each other and shook their heads.

We headed back to the cabins so TJ and Goose could get dried off. The adults saw us coming. TJ and Goose were soaked and went straight into the cabin while the adults looked at us, looked at the cousins, looked back at each other, then went back to the business at hand, while smiling.

I love camping with the cousins! I thought.

Lunchtime was quiet as everyone was glomming down their food. We gazed off into the woods and at the river, feeling better now that the campsite was set up and we had our first outdoor feast.

Shortly after lunch, we all agreed to go on a long hike in the mountains. We gathered at the beginning of the trail where TJ and Dexie led the way, much like Tarzan and Jane would lead expeditions to safety. Goose and I followed with the adults. The older cousins were dragging behind talking about the Beatles, astronauts, growing their hair, and their friends who were in the war.

It was hot out, but the trees shaded us just enough to keep cool as the pathway slowly inclined. We saw markers every now and then, confirming we were going in the right direction. There were a lot of twists and turns and fallen logs to jump over as we climbed our way higher.

The last leg of the hike was pretty steep and had a grassy incline that led to a lookout on a huge rock that overlooked the camp, streams, valleys, and peaks of the Pocono Mountains. TJ and Dexie raced to the top first, followed closely by Goose and me. The older cousins were next, taking long and careful strides to join us.

As the adults were catching up, my uncle Hank pushed past my dad and Uncle Foster, trying to get a lead. My father pulled the back of my uncle's shirt to ricochet past him. Uncle Foster wasn't having any of this as he pushed between his brothers while tripping them to their knees as he sped past, almost making it to the top.

They all didn't count on how steep and slippery the incline was. As Uncle Foster raised his arms in the air to break the imaginary ribbon at the top of the overlook, he slipped backward, rolling down the hill, knocking his brothers down again like bowling pins! They all skidded to a halt on their backs at the bottom of the incline. Startled and moaning, they looked up at my mom and aunts who were laughing uncontrollably looking down at them. It would have been a lot more embarrassing if not for the Ballantine cushion they had been working on since lunchtime.

Not long after, we were all at the top of the plateau, taking in the view and just talking in small pairs. Time didn't matter. We were here with family and the weather was perfect.

There was an occasional lull in the conversation to just relax and look out over the treetops and valleys to take it all in, and there was a lot to take in!

As the afternoon was slowly changing to early evening, we were ready to head back to camp. The younger cousins, led by Dexie, decided to slide down the steep slope by taking a running start, landing on their butts, and sliding down.

Dexie was going for the gold, looking like she was speeding down a snow-covered hill on an eighteen-wheeler's inner tube. Then she started to bounce and roll out of control. We all rolled and turned to miss hitting her.

She was abruptly stopped when her head and shoulder hit a gigantic oak tree and landed face down without moving. We all ran to get her. I got there first but didn't touch her in case her neck was injured. I learned that in the Cub Scouts. The cousins gathered around her as she started to roll over. There was blood dripping down her face, and she had a split lip. Mom and Dad made it down the hill and pushed through us with fear in their eyes. Mom saw the blood and screamed.

Dexie eventually opened her eyes, and with an enthusiastic smile, she yelled, "That was awesome!"

My aunt Marie told her to stay down and poured water from her canteen over the cuts on Dexie's face.

"Not too bad," they all agreed.

Just then, Dexie jumped up, wiped her lip with her wrist, and said, "Let's get going!" as if nothing had happened at all. No one was surprised. It was classic Dexie.

Everyone was relieved it was nothing serious, but Dexie was still confused as to why everyone was making such a big deal about it.

After a short rest to get over the Dexie incident, we headed back to camp and into our cabins. It was getting cooler so we all changed into our jeans and sweatshirts for the night.

The grills and firepit were lit as the sun began to set. No one was in a rush to eat as the grilled hot dogs, hamburgers, and baked beans slowly cooked. It was relaxing just watching the sun going down and the firepit getting brighter.

The food was laid out on the table. We didn't charge the food as expected; rather we took our time having a little bit here and there. Sitting around the firepit was holding our attention more. The cousins enjoyed water or Kool-Aid, and the moms joined the dads having some beer and smoking Marlboros and Kents around the campfire.

We listened to story after story from my parents, aunts, and uncles as we roasted marshmallows and just burned stuff. There was nothing better than pushing logs around in a fire with sturdy branches. We laughed, made fun, and ultimately started to doze off as the fire burned lower. It had been a long day.

The next morning, I woke up as the sun streamed into the cabin. Walking outside with a blanket wrapped around me, I saw that I was the last one to the party. The pans on the grill were sizzling with bacon, sausage links, and eggs, sunny side up! The older cousins and adults were having coffee. I grabbed a glass of orange juice and went to an empty spot at the table. The firepit was still smoldering from last night and the smoke combined with the smells in the mountain air were unbelievable. It was like everything was blooming all at once with all the best smells you have ever had.

We enjoyed a lazy day of swimming, digging for crayfish, playing horseshoes, and eating packaged snacks.

As the day went on, the adults began playing cards around the picnic tables. This left the cousins and me to gather across a shallow part of the river, then into the woods beyond, where we found a clearing and sat down on rocks, logs, and dirt hills.

Here was where it all happened.

Don and Kevin each pulled out two cans of beer that they snagged back at the campsite. They both had beer can openers on them. Hank and Shanda pulled out a pack of Marlboros while TJ pulled out two books of matches with our corner store deli emblem on them along with a pack of spearmint gum.

Dexie, Goose and I just looked at each other.

I said in a low voice, "Did I miss something?" They shrugged and joined in.

We all passed around the beers, puffed on cigarettes, and told wild stories. I took a sip and passed it along, trying not to make a distorted face from the taste. Goose drank it like it was Kool-Aid! I took a puff of a cigarette without inhaling and blew out some smoke. I passed it along to Goose, who tried making smoke rings then passed it to Dexie who did the same. Now I was thinking I was adopted.

The stories I heard about college life and the world in general were shocking. Everyone seemed to get it but me.

"Yeah, I'm definitely adopted," I said out loud. Of course, no one heard me.

This went on for hours as we all got to catch up and get to know each other a little bit better.

Before we left for the campsite, the older cousins told us to wash our faces and rinse our hair in the river as TJ handed out the spearmint gum.

"Good as new! No one will be the wiser," Don said as he led the way back to the cabins.

As early evening approached, my dad and uncles had their cars nearly loaded up. Sandwiches, chips, and drinks were handed out as we enjoyed one more meal together. Again, no one was in a rush. We didn't want the day to end.

The sun started to set as we hugged, kissed, shook hands, pushed, shoved, joked, and stared. Then we all got into our cars and headed home.

"I love camping with my cousins," I said as we pulled away.

Everyone in the car nodded and smiled.

CHAPTER 35

The Staff Start Returning

August 11

Giving teachers access to the school prior to their contractual date is synonymous with giving students their schedules weeks prior to opening day. They have way too much time to overanalyze things!

As I walked the hallways for my daily inspection of progress to the facility, the following comments of random staff members echoed off the walls:

- "Why did they move my room? That's not my room!"
- "That's not my chair! I bought a chair with my own money, and that's not my chair!"
- "So they're saying this year I'm on cafeteria duty? I made a deal three principals ago when I was hired that I would *never* have cafeteria duty!"
- "Who moved my cheese?"
- "Every year I order wall maps, and every year I get a calendar with a map of Manhattan on it!"
- "I would give anything to have my old overhead and opaque projectors back, please!"

- "I can't stay for the Back to School Night. Don't they know I'll miss *Jeopardy?*"
- "Second period prep? Why do they hate me?"
- "The band equipment and supplies haven't arrived yet. Our first competition is in four weeks! Camp is in two! They always favor sports!"
- "Could someone explain to Ms. Cattlevic that I do not share my classroom with anyone! Even though it's free four periods a day … my room. I've earned it. Remember Paul Greth the Meth! … They owe me!"
- "I have to be near a bathroom. They know I have to be near a … Oh sh@$ … I'll be right back!"
- "I'm pregnant. I'm going to be needing an expressing room … Private!"
- "I have changed my pronouns from *he* and *him* to *she* and *her.* I would like it announced at the welcome-back assembly so there's no doubt or confusion when I'm on duty in the locker rooms!"
- "Where are the new grievance forms?"

"Ahhh, gonna be a great school year. I can feel it!" I said to my office staff at the completion of my building tour.

No one looked up.

"Mrs. Lass, why are the phys ed and social studies teachers holding hands? Tell me they're not dating," I said.

Now the staff looked up.

"Where have you been?" she said in an amused way. "Been going on for six months now since he broke up with the board attorney."

"*What?*" I asked.

"Keep your eyes and ears open, Joe. That's all I'm sayin'. Keep your eyes and ears open!" Mrs. Lass repeated.

Glancing out at the parking lot, I saw five fifth graders

skateboarding. One boy stopped to stare in the window. The boy looked shocked that people were here. We could hear him screaming to his friends, "Why would anyone need to be in school over the summer? It's crazy!"

The boys left the parking lot confused.

The office staff, in unison, directed their attention to the conversations heard through the open main office doors.

"Do we have to wear ties this year? I will donate as much as it takes to have a no-tie day every day. I'm not a tie guy. I have rights, too, ya' know!"

"I have a new curriculum guide booklet. Could you hold it for me until the end of the year? I know I'll lose it."

"Anything good in them?"

"Nah. I was on the committee. Only cut and paste. The stipend was worth it, though!"

"I dragged a desk down the hallway. Not my desk! What a year already!"

"Hey! Who dug a scratch into the hallway floor with this desk?"

"Why did I come back today? Does anyone have Tums on them?"

The office staff glanced at each other, shook their heads with mild smiles, and continued working.

Some veteran staff came in today to poke around, get some inside scoop, and check out the new talent. Others dusted off the same old supplies, displays, and wall art they'd been using since Korvettes went out of business.

The sound of Mrs. Lass's voice rang over the PA system, cutting through the empty hallways.

"Please excuse the interruption. Would the owner of the bright red box truck blocking the main entrance doors please move it immediately?" she announced.

Within seconds, Mr. Epson, a nontenured English teacher,

raced into the office followed by Ms. Canon and Mr. Packard, two other nontenured members of the same department.

Mr. Epson began. "We're so sorry, Mrs. Lass. No disrespect intended. You see, the three of us work together at Staples in the summer because … well, you know … gotta keep the cash coming in! Anyway, as a favor, they let us have school supplies at a bigger discount and the manager is letting us use the truck to transport everything here. Is there a different spot we should park in?"

"We have some supplies in the closet. Did any of you order classroom equipment or supplies while we were doing budget requests last winter?" Mrs. Lass asked.

Ms. Canon answered with a smile and in a mild-mannered voice. "Yes, of course. And we just thought in addition to $38.12 each person in our department was allocated, we'd … ya' know … like to chip in, too! Why not order all the supplies for the entire year now rather than running out the second day of school?"

Mrs. Lass burst out laughing. "Best answer yet! Just move the truck up to the first visitor's spot. That should be fine."

In unison, they said, "Thank you, Mrs. Lass!"

Mrs. Lass then walked down the corridor and into the conference room as we were reviewing the resume of our first interview of the afternoon.

"Your 1:00 p.m. interview is in the main office, Dr. Strat, but Iggy would like a word with you first," Mrs. Lass said. "What should I tell him?"

"Have him come in, Mrs. Lass," I answered.

Iggy came in shaking his head and ready to explode.

"Good afternoon, Iggy!" I said cheerfully, anticipating a blowup. "What can I help you with?"

"Dr. Strat, there are only twelve teachers here to set up their rooms. Look at the floors! Look at the mess! Are we going to keep doing this for the next few weeks while I have a building to get ready?"

"Iggy, we do this every year. The building looks great. We can't keep the teachers out. I'll have a word with them when they come in each day. I'll even send an email for them to be careful and considerate as they go through the building. Good?" I asked.

"Ahhh, the school is so much more manageable without the teachers and students in it," Iggy responded, not necessarily happy.

As Iggy left the conference room, the committee looked at each other shaking their heads in agreement.

We spent the remainder of the afternoon interviewing two final candidates.

As 3:30 p.m. approached, I shouted, "Another week in the books! Let's lock up!"

The staff moved at a slow, end-of-the-week pace.

"If anyone wants to meet at Jazzy's, first round is on me!" I shouted a little louder.

The pace picked up tremendously as we locked up and all met at Jazzy's ten minutes later.

Once there, we sat at two long tables pulled together in the back and started our happy hour. The bartender seemed to be the only one covering the room so he came to the table and took our drink orders. I hadn't seen him before. He said his name was Matt. He was middle-aged, had dark-brown hair with a couple of grays coming through, and was clean-shaven.

I followed him back to the bar to make certain I pay for the first round—and to add a couple of appetizers to the list. He sent the order into the kitchen then began making the drinks.

"Are you new here, Matt?" I asked.

"Sort of. I grew up here then moved to Florida. My daughter Tess lives here and we don't get to see her much, so my wife and I decided to move back," he said.

"So here you are," I said.

"Well, for now. My wife and I are opening a cafe and bookstore in town. It's being renovated this month. My lease starts in September," he said in a nervous voice.

"So family run! I'm jealous. I've always wanted to open a bookstore. I love to read, write, and have always felt at home in a bookstore," I said.

"Same here. But my wife and I will run the store. My daughter just got her master's degree and is currently looking for a job," Matt said.

"What's her degree in?" I asked.

"Advanced mathematics," Matt said proudly. "She's a teacher."

Before he could say another word, I slipped him my card and begged—uh, asked—him to ask if she would be interested in giving me a call about the AP calculus vacancy. With a huge grin, he tucked the card into the front pocket of his shirt and thanked me for the lead.

By the time I got back to the table, the appetizers were being served. Matt brought the first round just in time.

I made a toast. "To another great year, with a great group of educators … Oh, and you guys, too!"

The usual moans, groans, and laughter followed.

"Seriously, though. We've got a lot left to do in a short period of time. But for now, the weekend begins. Let's drink!" I said with my glass lifted.

"Here, here!" The rest joined in.

You could tell a little about a person by the drink they ordered. Mrs. Lass? Gin and tonic. Ms. Cattlevic? Cabernet. Mrs. Keller? Moscow mule. Ms. Sharp? Fireball. Ms. Frenzy? Fireball. Coach Slick? Draft beer. Me? Bourbon, of course.

As it got close to 5:30 p.m., we said our goodbyes and headed home. I had a weekend of yard work, painting, and paying bills to look forward to.

A lot was accomplished this past week. I was feeling good about the upcoming opening of the school year. But I would be fooling myself if I didn't say I was getting more exhausted as each summer went by. It was not easy to admit that you were getting older. Or as I liked to say, more veteran, established, experienced. Yup, gettin' older.

CHAPTER 36

Ellen

August 4, 1964

For a Tuesday night, it was kind of quiet. My friends were either home or out with their families. There was a little light left to the day so I jumped on my Schwinn and rode down to the corner deli for a roll of butterscotch Life Savers and a Coke.

As I was paying for my after-dinner snack, I heard a familiar voice behind me. "Hi, Joey!" I felt a tap on my shoulder.

It was Ellen, with her brother Yeffie by her side.

"Oh hi, Ellen … Yeffie! What are you doin' here?" I said, just to say something.

"Yeffie and I have to get a carton of Marlboros and three gallons of milk for Mom," she said, rolling her eyes. "I can't carry it all on my own."

"Yeah, I'm just here to get some snacks before it gets dark out," I said shyly.

We gathered our supplies, went to the counter, and paid for our stuff then walked out into the parking lot together. The sun was beginning to set.

Ellen had always been easy to talk to. We even dressed in the same costumes as bums for the school's Halloween parade last year. I'd never hear the end of it from my friends. That was when we really started talking … ya' know?

Our parents had been friends since we moved into town. We affectionately called them Aunt Shannon and Uncle Jessie, even though we were not related. Aunt Shannon cooked all day, and Uncle Jessie was a lawyer. I'd never seen all of her brothers and sisters together since there were thirteen of them. I was not sure she had either.

Ellen had been in my class since kindergarten, and Yeffie was a grade older. His name was really Jeffrey, but when he was younger, all he could say when anyone asked his name was Yeffie. That was how it started, I guess.

Yeffie seemed to be in a hurry to get home. Ellen, not so much.

"Do you know who your teacher is next year?" she asked.

"Nah, you?" I answered.

"No," she replied.

"I hope it's not Ms. Obdurate!" we said at the same time. "Jinx!" again together.

We laughed. Yeffie didn't. He was carrying the milk.

"Let's go, Ellen!" he said as he nudged her to move on.

"You can start goin'. I'll catch up," she said.

Yeffie started walking while shaking his head.

"I guess school will be starting pretty soon. The summer goes by fast, huh?" Ellen said, hoping to keep the conversation going.

"Too fast for me," I said with a smile on my face.

There was a short silence as we both looked down at the ground.

"Well, I should get going too," she said shyly while grinning. "I'll see you soon, OK?" she asked.

I nodded with a smile.

It all happened so fast! I couldn't remember a thing, but I could remember everything. It was quick but in slow motion.

All I remembered was that she kissed me! Right on the lips! She giggled, smiled, and waved goodbye, all at the same time.

I sat down immediately on one of the milk crates against the deli wall as she caught up to Yeffie, looking back twice with a huge smile.

A good five minutes went by before I felt confident enough to stand up straight without embarrassing myself. It was getting dark out. I looked left, looked right, then hopped on my bike and headed home.

Once inside, I ran upstairs into my room, turned on the lights, and headed to my dresser. I stared into the mirror with my heart still pounding and a look of confusion on my face. After a few deep breaths, reality set in. A smile started to form on my face that got bigger ... bigger ...

"Yes!" I shouted. "Yes, yes, yeeeees!"

I really didn't know what just happed. This was all new to me.

I fell back on my bed and stared at the ceiling, replaying what happened over and over and over again. What a strange feeling.

Then terror struck! *"What am I going to do the next time I see her?"* I groaned.

CHAPTER 37

Board Approval

August 15

Our Tuesday morning meeting covered a lot of ground. We would seal the deal on four vacancies for board approval at tonight's meeting. If they were approved, three would begin on September 1, and one was being held to sixty-day notice.

An interim director of guidance, Dr. Winfrey, would also begin on Monday morning for a two-week crossover with Mrs. Keller. She had a great reputation as a leader and had recently retired.

The board would also approve the updated curriculum. Superintendent Fieldman would footnote the definition of curriculum on the bottom of the meeting agenda for those board members who may not understand what *curriculum* meant. She would also read the definition for those members who may be literacy challenged.

Other agenda items would include the following:

- approving district textbooks, which may or may not exist,

- approving the athlete curricular and extracurricular inventory, which may or may not be accurate,
- approving the food service provider, with the stipulation they show documentation of where they really get their food and if it was indeed consumable,
- approval of out-of-district placements (This usually went quickly with a unanimous vote since the board was still confused as to what it was.),
- approval of individual staff professional development opportunities (This usually took the most time because the board members felt if the staff had degrees in their field, why would they need to miss a workday for something they should already know? And why should the board have to pay for it?),
- approval to dispose of obsolete equipment (Board members asked, "Did we try selling this equipment on eBay? Let's use our heads!"),
- approval of additional period assignments (Board members asked, "We're paying for this?), and
- approval of extracurricular stipend positions (Board members asked many questions, including these:

"Why are we paying so much money for these positions?"

- "If the teachers are dedicated, they should do it for free. Did you ask them?"
- "Do we need all these activities? I mean not including sports?"
- "These teachers are getting away with murder!"
- "What is FBLA?"

- "We have an LGBTQ Club? And we're paying for it?
- And the final agenda item was approval of the revised board policy's first reading. It was "Policy: NCC-1701 Dress Code: Teaching staff will only wear outfits in school colors."

Unless requested, I would try not to be available for the August General Board of Education meetings.

CHAPTER 38

Junkyard Gold!

August 11, 1964

Tuesday morning was the best day of the week to rummage through the junkyard next to the railroad tracks just a block past the ball fields. Especially in August when everyone was throwing out good stuff before the fall. Roger, Goose, and I began at the newly discarded section of the buffet.

"I can't believe people throw this stuff out!" I shouted to the other two.

"Me neither!" Roger shouted back.

Goose just continued to climb up the pile of junk like we were playing king of the hill. We tossed around old bike parts, sinks, tables, chairs, dolls, and rusted lawn furniture. Goose put an old bucket over his head with a broken umbrella in his hand.

"Look! I'm Errol Flynn!" He laughed as he pretended to ward off the bad guys.

"More like Brother Dim!" Roger fired back.

I saw an old box of spark plugs, empty oil cans, and pieces of a broken carburetor.

This is getting good! I thought.

Underneath the boxes were more motor parts and a rusted

monkey wrench. I dug deeper, tossing aside a shredded winter jacket and a well-stained blanket. At the same time, Roger brushed dirt off a bright pink Sunday church hat and put it on his head. He danced around doing his best Mae West impression, saying, "Hey, boys. Come up and see me sometime!"

Goose and I just shook our heads, then busted out laughing.

Roger and Bud kept searching and found two bent badminton rackets sticking out of a new pile of trash and immediately began smacking golf ball-size rocks at each other. That lasted a few swings until the rackets completely fell apart.

I continued to dig then hit something hard, bending back my thumb nail. I screamed a few well-chosen four-letter words then checked out the damage … Not too bad.

Back to the business at hand. I cleared the area around the object like I was scooping sand from around a pirate's chest. There it was. I couldn't believe my eyes! Could it be? No … no. A little more scooping then … I thought, *Holy* … "Motherlode!" I screamed. "Motherlode!"

There it was. Like a block of solid gold. I gazed at it in disbelief. But there it was! I can swear I heard a choir of angels singing from above as my eyes swelled with tears. Roger and Goose ran as fast as they could then froze and gasped. All three sets of eyes stared down in reverence with mouths wide-open. Yes … yes … It was a two-and-a-half-horsepower, solid-black side shaft Briggs & Stratton motor!

"Do you have any idea what this is?" I said, as if whispering in church. "We can build a motorbike! A motorbike!" I shouted, barely containing my enthusiasm.

The others were equally shocked at this find.

We lifted the treasure out and away from the other ordinary garbage and placed it down carefully on the path. There we just stared and marveled.

"It looks like it's in good shape," Roger said as we wiped it clean with the bottom of our shirts. "It's beautiful!"

I ran to get my bike. Then Roger and Goose lifted the motor onto the base of my handlebars.

I rode slowly with one hand securing the motor as we all headed for my house. We managed to get it to my backyard without incident, where we dismounted our prize onto the grass then sat in a circle around it to take it all in.

"Does it work?" Goose asked.

"I doubt it will start, but let's give it a try," I replied, knowing there was no way it would.

We put a little fresh gas in the tank, and each took turns pulling the recoil starter rope.

"The piston is going up and down so it's not frozen," I said. "Not even close to starting. We should take it apart and clean it. My dad has tools in the basement."

Goose and I went downstairs and grabbed some crescent wrenches, screwdrivers, and rags. We were not new to working on small motors. TJ invites us to help take apart and clean out our lawnmower motor at the end of every summer. This came naturally to him. We all had advanced degrees in kid motor repairs. Even at our age.

We lifted the motor and placed it gently on an old piece of plywood by the metal shed in the back of our yard. I carefully unscrewed the carburetor then began to loosen the bolts of the head. We dropped the carburetor into a large coffee can half filled with gasoline. TJ had told us on more than one occasion that this would clean out the inside.

Once the head was off, we saw all the carbon caked on the piston and the underside of the head. The spark plug was a block of black gunk. We cleaned everything the only way we knew how: by scraping all the black off the piston and motorhead with screwdrivers. A rag dipped in gas cleaned off the rest. The gas tank was rinsed out with fresh gas then emptied. The filter was hard and black so we rinsed it in gas, like a sponge, until the black was gone.

"The spark plug is shot," Roger said.

"There's a box of them in the junkyard. I saw 'em. We need a game plan. Remember the motorbike the older kids down the block built last year?" I asked.

Roger said, "Yeah. So we need to find a washing machine pulley for the back tire rim, a belt, a steel angle bar to set the motor on, and a three-speed handlebar grip and cable to use as a throttle. Oh yeah, and a small shaft pulley."

"Is that all?" Goose mocked.

"Hey, TJ has some stuff around here. And we can sift through the junkyard for the rest. We're wasting time! Let's go!" I said.

We hopped on our bikes and headed back to the junk buffet with a wrench, pliers, screwdriver, and hammer. We arrived knowing what came first. We needed to go around to the back where the old appliances were dumped.

There were three ancient washing machines crushed against an old oak tree. We checked carefully. The motor was missing on the first one. The second one had already been stripped for parts, and the third one was under the other two.

Between the three of us, we managed to push the first two off the bottom washer. We could see through the split open back that the twelve-inch pulley was still connected to the drum underneath. With our tools, pieces of metal, and sharp rocks lying around the dump, we ripped open the shell of the washer enough to get to the pulley. For the next half hour, we tried to unbolt the pulley from the motor and drum.

"I love this stuff!" I said out loud. The others nodded in agreement.

With a lot of determination, and a few scrapes and bruises, we finally unbolted the pulley and tugged it free. It was in great shape and just the right size to bolt, with washers, to the spokes of a back wheel.

With this success, we headed back to my house to drop off the pulley and tools. It was hot and getting hotter out. Too hot to continue this project. Too hot for a pickup baseball game. It was definitely a lake afternoon. Roger and Goose agreed.

We stopped off to see if the gang was around. Only Micky was home, and he came with us. Along the way, we saw Tommy throwing a rubber ball against the dugout wall. He saw what we were up to and joined in. The motorbike could wait. It was time to cool off.

We headed to the lake, where we ran into other friends from school, and spent the rest of the afternoon embarrassing ourselves on the diving boards doing belly flops and attempting flips. Out of the corner of my eye, I saw Ellen and her friends. She waved to me with a bright smile. I waved back, trying to look casual and cool. Then I quickly went into the lake waist deep. It would be quite a while before I could get out of the water without more embarrassment.

CHAPTER 39

September Is Coming Up Fast!

August 16

It was a clear and calm Wednesday morning so I decided to take my Harley-Davidson to work. I promised myself each summer that I would ride more. And each summer, there was so little time that I only got a few rides in.

I was greeted at the front door by Coach Slick. "Hey there, Easy Rider. Is that a leather tie? Got the hog tied up out front? Your gang let you solo today?" was his greeting.

"Good morning, Coach," I replied. "Take your little comfy Pinto to work today?"

"Hey, hey! A little respect. Gremlin … But point well taken," Coach said. "We're scrimmaging at one o'clock, home field, if you can stop by. Support the team!"

"I'll try to stop by," I answered.

He replied, "Gonna get our butts kicked!"

"We're gonna miss you around here, Coach," I said.

He smiled, then thought about what I said. But by the time he turned back to say something, I was already stepping into the office.

"Good morning, all!" I said.

"Good morning, Killer!" Mrs. Lass said with her usual uplifting smile. "Want a security detail around that scooter?"

So much for enjoying a morning ride.

"Can I get anyone coffee?" I offered.

A few takers followed me into the office. Best way to get the weekend scoop ... and then some.

A half hour later, Ms. Cattlevic, Mrs. Lass, and I put together the agenda for our 10:00 a.m. meeting. Reagan has done her homework, as usual. She set up detailed instructions for our upcoming freshmen orientation, new teacher orientation, and luncheon and put together an outline of an agenda for the staff's first day back.

"Did you get any time for yourself this weekend?" I asked while looking through the outlines.

"A little," she said. "Love doing this. Once I start, I have to finish."

Mrs. Lass and I shared a glance and smile.

"You left nothing for us to do!" I said with a big grin.

"Don't listen to him, Ms. Cattlevic. He never did it anyway!" she joked.

"Coffee?" I asked, quickly changing the subject.

"He's good at that," Mrs. Lass fired back. "Getting coffee, I mean."

We all laughed.

"Seriously. Great job!" I said in a sincere tone.

"That's what I'm here for, boss!" she said in an appreciative voice.

"Boss?" Mrs. Lass asked. "That's gonna go to his head."

She was on a roll.

We finalized the details of today's agenda items. Mrs. Lass ran off copies as well as emailed the agendas to the team. The three of us then stopped by Mrs. Keller's office to officially welcome aboard our new interim director of guidance, Dr. Winfrey, who was already wrist deep in paperwork. Mrs. Keller was smiling an "I see the light at the end of the tunnel" smile.

Coach Slick popped his head in and said, "Hey, welcome aboard. The football team from your last district destroyed us! You gonna wear our school colors now?"

"Any free attire you can get me, I'll wear," she joked, with a big smile on her face.

"I like her!" Coach said. Then he disappeared.

"I think you'll enjoy your time with us," I said. "Colorful bunch!"

Dr. Winfrey nodded. "I'm sure."

She and Mrs. Keller went back to work. It appeared she was leading the conversation more than Mrs. Keller was.

More and more teachers were coming in to set up their rooms. It was good to see their faces again. All in all, they were smiling and joking with the office staff looking eager to get back. They talked briefly about their vacations, families, summer jobs, and how short the summer was and that they couldn't believe it was almost over. Then of course, reality set in as they began requesting supplies they forgot to order and grumbling about their needs for special accommodations if they were to be successful this year.

Mrs. Lass and Ms. Frenzy ran interference, addressing each of their concerns so Reagan and I could prepare for our meeting. Iggy slipped by them to offer his daily complaints directly to me. I listened, nodded, gave him a cup of coffee, and sent him on his way.

Our meeting started at 10:00 sharp. I began by detailing our upcoming events and time frames. The team was noticeably back in full swing, taking notes, asking pertinent questions, and offering positive comments.

Ms. Cattlevic took over, delineating the programs we needed to finalize in the upcoming weeks. The staff responded to her as if she'd been on the team for years. Respect for her position and as a person was immediate. Especially after the Sycoe incident.

"I would like to address the building walk-through inspection Ms. Cattlevic and I did yesterday afternoon," I said. "Mrs. Lass, could you call Iggy in for this? Thank you."

"There are ants coming out of the main hallway girls' bathroom drain. Iggy? What's the deal?" I asked.

"On it. Flushing it, cleaning it, a little special chemical. Perfectly safe. Next?" he responded, trying to deflect further inquiries.

I'll need to address this later with Iggy, in private.

"There are dead cockroaches in the band practice rooms. I thought we exterminated," I continued.

"Two new freshmen flute players brought them from home. They said the roaches were their pets. I guess they didn't know about the exterminators," he said while staring at the floor with his head tilted and a smirk on his face.

Everyone briefly shifted their eyes at each other, then I continued.

"The exploded toilet in the locker room from graduation night is still not fixed. Iggy? Coach?"

Coach jumped in saying, "Iggy and I thought it would be better to replace it the last week of August, just in case there are any copycat board member attacks."

"Coach, all the gym doors to the outside were propped open again. An escapee from the senior assisted living facility was sitting in the center of the basketball court meditating, and nobody did anything. Just walked around her!" I said, staring directly at him.

Coach responded quickly. "Uh, well, heh, I'll uh have to get on that right away. I told those guys—"

"Gonna miss you around here, Coach," I said, now looking back at the agenda.

Coach said, "That's the second time you—"

I continued. "Next there are three boxes filled with antique computer parts in the hallway outside of your office, Mr. Jopps. Keeping? Throwing out? What?"

Mr. Jopps spoke softly, shaking his head mildly up and down with his eyes closed and a smile on his face. "Well, if you knew the history of the components, and the—"

Before he continued, I politely interrupted. "Don't start, Mr. Jopps. Just get them out of the hallway, all right?"

"Yes, sir!" he answered with his eyes now open.

"Iggy," I said, "the mini fridge in the science lab storage area has a bad seal. Nobody noticed the stench. There are two moldy piglets and a pile of frog parts inside."

Without looking up, Iggy said, "On it. One of the first rooms we cleaned at the start of the summer. Sorry."

I took a sip of coffee then directed my attention to Coach. "Coach, the phys ed teacher's office is just—do something with it. It's disgusting!"

Coach answered, "I never noticed … Don't say it!"

I just shook my head.

"Iggy. Your cleaning crew is in the teachers' lounge every day. They never mentioned the cracked and stained ceiling tile with the squirrel's nest peeking out. No one?" I asked.

"Well … You make it sound like nothing is getting done. We work pretty—" Iggy began.

"Just fix it. Please," I said.

"Got it," he replied.

Looking around the table, I said, "The picnic tables are piled on top of each other in the courtyard again. Can't we chain those things down! Anyone? And can we clear the empty beer cans off the roof before they all blow into the parking lot? People, we need eyes!"

The team looked at each other trying not to be noticed or picked on.

Also, I continued. "There's a container of putrid green liquid in the file room. How long has that been sitting in there?"

Mrs. Keller shyly responded, "That's my breakfast!"

Couldn't stop the laughter if we tried.

As the meeting ended, I said, "Lastly, our districtwide administrative retreat and professional development day will be held this Friday."

Groans went all around.

"The board will be providing breakfast and lunch," I added.

"I hope the food's good!" someone shouted.

"No guarantees," I said. "All right. Let's get to work!"

For lunch, I had a protein bar and coffee. It was the easiest thing I could bring on the Harley. Afterward, I stopped by to see how the football team was doing. The score was 48–0, visitors leading. I watched about fifteen minutes of the massacre. It was like watching the Justice League play against the Three Stooges. The coaches waved to me from the field. In turn, I gave a thumbs up and began to mentally write the vacancy ads for next year's coaching staff.

When I arrived at my office the next morning, Thursday, August 17, I scanned the calendar and saw that there was a meeting with our local law enforcement command across town.

There was a light rain falling as Harriet, Reagan and I drove to the township's municipal building. We would be gathering at 11:00 a.m. with Police Chief Nimoy and Captain Pike for our annual meeting regarding our "Memorandum of Agreement."

The MOA was the agreement between the school district and our local law enforcement agency detailing the responsibilities of each as mandated by the state. This lengthy document was the backbone of the understanding as to who did what, where, when, and how. I actually hadn't gotten around to reading it, and I believed this may be the same for Harriet. Captain Pike may have, and I was pretty sure the chief couldn't read. It was nice to get together, though.

We reviewed our protocols over coffee and bagels and caught up on family, friends, criminals, future criminals from the graduating class and staff, and other important topics. I formally introduced Reagan at the beginning of the meeting. She had been a great part of our discussion, as if she'd been to these meetings before.

After a few final jokes about the locals, the chief asked if we needed to cover any specifics he may have missed.

In a very supportive and positive manner, Reagan asked, "Chief could you please clarify for me the …"

Chief Nimoy, Captain Pike, Harriet, and I looked at each other with the same thought. She read the "Memorandum of Agreement."

I'm pretty sure she knew we didn't read it, and we were now certain that she did. However, the skill it took for her to guide us and clarify each of our responsibilities, while simultaneously making it seem like it was the other way around, was masterful! Bravo!

We all left the meeting happy, smiling, shaking hands, and wishing for another great school year working together. All this while being schooled by the new kid. And not even knowing it!

At the end of the day, I hopped on my Harley and took the long way home through the back roads. No one was on the roads. Just the way I liked it. I needed more time to enjoy the little things in life. This was one of them.

CHAPTER 40

The Motorbike

August 12, 1964

"Where did you get that motor?" TJ screamed as he jumped on me, waking me up on a cloudy Thursday morning. Goose saw a chance for a pile on and joined in. Just because.

"Come on. Come on. Come on! Where did you get it!" TJ persisted.

"In the junkyard. You missed it! It was buried with all the new Tuesday stuff," I said while smirking proudly.

"Nooooo!" TJ shouted while dropping to the floor for effect. He immediately sat straight up and continued. "I'll give you five bucks for it!"

"One hundred dollars!" I said with a straight face, but I was laughing and loving it on the inside.

"You're crazy! Seven bucks," he fired back.

"Nope!" I said in complete control of the situation.

Excitedly TJ asked, "Does it work?"

Grinning, I said, "No."

Goose interrupted. "I'm hungry."

TJ asked, "Did you clean the carburetor?"

I said, "Of course I did."

Goose interrupted again. "I want cereal."

TJ went on. "So what are you gonna do with it?"

I told him, "Roger, Goose, and I are building a motorbike."

Goose said, "It needs a spark plug ... and a lot of stuff."

Looking surprised, TJ said, *"Roger, too?"*

I told him, "We found it together."

Goose added, "I wore a bucket on my head."

We both looked at Goose without saying a word, then I continued. "We're trying to find all the pieces we need. Already have a pulley for the back wheel. Saw a twenty-inch frame and a front rim in the junkyard. The tire is bald and it's flat, but we could patch the tube."

TJ quickly answered, "My friends and I have some stuff. I know we can get the motor running. If we partner up, we can get this thing going in no time!"

Trying to remain in control, I said, "Let me think about it ... Goose?"

Goose answered, "I don't care."

I looked back at TJ and said, with my best businessman face, "I'll run it by Roger, but I really found the motor so I get the first test ride!"

TJ said, while extending his hand, "Then it's a deal!"

I stuck out my hand and said, "Deal!"

Goose stuck out his hand and said, "Deal!"

By early afternoon, Roger, Goose, and I met up with TJ and his buddies Barrett and Jake. Barrett was taller than all of us, and Jake had bright red hair. Couldn't miss either of them in a crowd. Between the three of them, they brought a back wheel with an inflated tire, an angle bar, and a three-speed throttle and cable.

"OK, what else do we need to find?" I asked the group.

That was when Roger opened a small toolbox containing an electric drill, nuts, bolts, washers, and ... a spark plug. Compliments of his father ... if his father knew ...

TJ, Roger, Goose, and I started assembling the motor. TJ did the majority of the work but showed us what he was doing step by step. He explained to us that the carburetor had jets that needed to be cleaned out for the fuel mixture. Goose took a shot at cleaning the pin tiny ports with, of course, a pin. The gasoline the carburetor was soaking in cleaned out the bigger parts.

It took a while, but once the carburetor was together, I screwed it into the motor with a gasket we made out of melted-down, two-inch, little, green army men. Roger bolted the head on while Goose filled the block with oil. TJ replaced the filter with one my father had in the shed.

There was no exhaust on it when we found it so Barrett went back home to get several threaded pipes his father had in his garage. His father was a plumber so we had a good amount of five-inch threaded pipes to try to make it work.

The fourth pipe was a perfect fit. Jake said stuffing some steel wool in it would quiet the noise of the motor. We put enough in, but not too much.

I had the honor of attaching the spark plug to the head and then the wire to the spark plug. TJ filled the tank with fresh gas from my father's tin gas can. We were ready to give it a go. The others circled around to witness this historic event.

I pulled the starter cord. The sound of the motor chugged but with no life.

Another pull. Still not starting.

TJ made small adjustments to what he said was the mixture screw on the side of the carburetor after each of the next four pulls.

The fifth pull brought brief life to our treasure. The excitement mounted.

The next pull led to a few seconds of running with some smoke coming out of the exhaust pipe. More excitement.

One more pull and the motor came to life, but wheezing like it had asthma. Jake grabbed the screwdriver and slowly adjusted the mixture screw like a surgeon. Smoother … Smoother …

"It's alive! It's alive!" we shouted in triumph.

What a feeling! We did it! We were all out of breath from cheering but still smiling.

We let the motor run at a low speed for the next five minutes just to break it in. Meanwhile, we saw the progress Barrett and Jake had made on the frame.

They drilled six holes in a circle around the washing machine pulley. Using the wide washers, nuts, and bolts Roger brought over, they connected the pulley to the back tire rim by using the washers to attach the spokes of the back wheel to the pulley. It looked pretty centered for a first try.

They not only attached the back tire to the frame of the bike but had also fixed the flat on the front tire and attached it to the forks. Jake found rusted monkey bars that he cleaned up and attached to the frame. An old banana seat wrapped in duct tape would do for now. It actually looked like a motorbike. Mean-looking. No pedals were needed. We had a motor!

The next step was to connect the ninety-degree angle bar horizontally onto the right side of the frame, drilling into the angle bar and frame just above where the pedals would be. This took a while as well as three different drill bits.

Once the drilling was completed, the angle bar was attached to the bicycle frame with nuts, bolts, and washers. A vision to behold!

Next the motor was lifted and placed gently on the angle bar by me and TJ as we lined up the holes and bolted the left side of the motor block to the angle bar.

Perfect fit!

Then Jake bolted a brace from the head of the engine to the frame crossbar for strength and stability. It looked insane!

It would be easy to ride with your left hand on the handlebars and your right hand on the accelerator of the motor for speed control. But this design would be a little sloppy and not so ... cool. TJ said an easy fix was to take the steel ball out of the three-speed gear changer. This made it a smooth throttle rather than clicking for each gear.

I attached the handlebar grip throttle to the handlebar and the cable that ran to the motor accelerator and duct-taped the cable onto the crossbar. Goose added a few drops of oil into the cable casing then turned the throttle several times to smooth out the roughness.

The only items left were a pulley for the front motor shaft and a belt that would fit around the distance of the front and back pulleys. Problem was we didn't have a front pulley and we would have to buy the right belt from the Esso station around the corner.

TJ said a standard four-inch pulley was hard to find. It also limited us to running with the motorbike to jumpstart it since the wheels and pulleys would be directly attached to the motor. Going faster was not a problem. But the slower you went, the slower the engine would go until it stalled out. Either way, by tomorrow morning we hoped to have found a pulley to get this chopper on the road! Not legally, but on the road.

After a quick ten-second dinner, I raced out the front door to meet up with my friends at the end of the driveway. We knew what each of us had for dinner by the fresh stains on our T-shirts.

We rode around the driveway in figure eights, ready to go pulley shopping at the junkyard buffet when a group of the older kids from the higher numbers on our street headed into our neighborhood in formation on their bikes. The seven of them circled the five of us. We looked at each other and then glanced at our houses to see if we had backup in the event of trouble.

"TJ told us you're building a motorbike," the leader said. I thought his name was Neil.

"Yeah," I replied in a cautious tone, trying to read their facial expressions. "It's coming along."

"Your brother said you were looking for a front shaft pulley. Did you find one yet?" Neil asked.

"No, but we're heading back to the junkyard now. I'm sure we'll find one," I said confidently.

The kid on the bike to the left of Neil, I think his name was Buzz, looked at us with a smile and said, "So I guess you won't be needing this?"

Buzz turned his left palm up not only to display a pulley, but a centrifugal clutch pulley!

A centrifugal clutch let the motor shaft spin while not engaging. The faster the engine went, the more the clutch engaged, making the motorbike move. We'd seen pictures of one, but never in real life!

We all just stared saying, "No way!"

"How much?" I started to negotiate.

Neil glanced at the others and then directly at Buzz, who looked down at the clutch and said, "It's yours!"

We couldn't believe it. Free!

"With the following conditions," he continued.

All our faces dropped. *Here it comes,* I thought. *Too good to be true.*

He got off his bike, walked over to me, and put the clutch in my hand saying, "We get to try it out when it's done."

We all nodded our heads. That was not such a high price to pay for an amazing clutch.

"And," he concluded, staring at my house with a shy grin." I thought, *Here we go ...* "Tell Dexie we let you have it."

"That's it? OK, you got it!"

We shook hands to seal the deal then headed back to our upper and lower numbered neighborhoods.

Once we were in my backyard again, we slipped the clutch loosely on the motor shaft to align it with the back pulley.

"Good fit!" I said.

We then measured, with a piece of rope, to determine which size belt we needed to connect the pulley just as TJ came out the back door to join us.

"You got the pulley," he said, not surprised at all. "Good!"

"You knew they were going to give us the clutch?" Roger asked, very confused.

"Not for sure, but I thought they might," TJ said with a smirk.

"They said they wanted to try it out when it was running. They also said to tell Dexie that they gave it to us," I said. "Why would they say that?"

Now I was more confused.

TJ just stared me down with that big grin on his face. I looked at the others. They were looking down and trying not to smile.

What am I missing? I thought.

Just then, I thought of Ellen. I looked up and said, "Ohhhhhh!"

The others said, "Yeeeeeah!"

"Those guys don't know what they're in for!" I said while shaking my head.

We all laughed in agreement.

TJ said, "That's their problem!"

We laughed even louder as we began to walk to the Esso station for the belt. The final piece to the puzzle.

The next morning, after breakfast, we all met in my backyard and put the belt on.

It fit, first try!

We pulled the back tire for just enough tension on the belt then tightened both bolts to the frame.

As agreed, I got the first solo ride. I hopped on that magnificent chopper and pulled the cord. There was a promising chug.

I pulled the cord two more times before the motor fired up.

Cheers all around.

I balanced the motorbike toward the road then twisted the

throttle inward slowly to give it some gas. The bike crept forward. A little more throttle and I was riding!

The tension and anxiety left my body. The feeling couldn't be explained in words. I rode it up and down the driveway a few times to get my balance then took it on the road. First stop, the upper numbers, where the older kids were gathered on Neil's front yard.

The sound of the motor brought them to the street. I rode by them with a victorious smile on my face, circled around, and stopped in front of them. They all cheered and started patting me on the back. Again, couldn't explain the feeling.

As promised, they each took a turn riding it up and down the road. Cheers from the low numbers, then the upper numbers. When they were done, more back patting and congratulations. I thanked them again for their help then headed back home. The seven of us took turns riding up and down the road, carefully looking out for cops as we went.

Dexie came out to see what all the commotion was about. She stared at the motorbike, looked at us, and asked, "Can I have a turn?"

How could we say no? If it weren't for her, we wouldn't be riding.

As she mounted up, I said, "By the way, Buzz and his friends wanted us to tell you that they gave us the clutch for free! If it weren't for them, we'd be stuck."

She smiled that knowing smile and took off onto the road to the upper numbers. We saw her stop in front of Neil's house. She was talking to them for about a half hour before we saw her, or the motorbike, again.

"I guess she's thanking them," I said.

The others just shook their heads and smiled.

CHAPTER 41

Kumbaya Day

August 18

My wife and I became close friends with the superintendent, Harriet Fieldman, and her husband, Cory. She was well respected around the state, and he was an artist and an avid fisherman. We'd been invited several times on their boat, *The Party Penguin!* I was not much of a fisherman, but I loved spending time with good friends.

As I always said, "Half the people hate the principal; everyone hates the superintendent!"

However, our professional relationship was similar with a mutual respect for our positions.

That being said, I hated superintendent round table meetings, and I especially hated these districtwide administrative retreat and professional development days each summer.

The meeting was held at Harriet's office on the far north end of town that might as well have been located on a private island. It was a stark-looking building at the end of a dead-end road. There was a one-foot-by-two-foot sign five feet from the right side of the off-centered front door that simply read, "Board Office." I scanned my district ID and rang the buzzer. I was greeted by a staticky voice asking who I was. I looked directly into the security camera and responded, "Principal Strat."

"Are you here for the meeting?" the voice asked.

Amused and confused by the question, I responded, "Yes."

The buzzer to enter lasted long enough for me to pull the door open.

I walked down the narrow, dimly lit hallway past a faded, windowless door on the left. That was the business administrator's office. I continued to the end of the hallway to a door with a smoked glass window and a brass nameplate overhead that read, "Superintendent's Office."

After pressing one more buzzer, the door clicked open for me to enter.

The reception area was the size of a classroom, well-lit, air-conditioned, with classical music playing softly in the background. Harriet's assistant, Ms. Shondella, was a cheery women in her thirties. She stood up to greet me then guided me to the board's conference room. Most of the administrative team was already seated around the twenty-five-foot, solid-oak conference table in this palatial, professionally decorated room facing a glass wall overlooking an angel fountain feature and the densely wooded private property. Harriet's even larger office was located through the door on the left.

Rumor had it that when the building was first constructed, the superintendent's office was called the think tank. Well, it supposedly housed an eight-seat Jacuzzi. One of the nine board members had to sit out in case the other eight drowned. That person would be the sole survivor to carry on the district's mission.

The day began with happy faces as the district administrative team got their coffee, tea, bagels, Excedrin, NoDoz, and CBD gummies. We were instructed to wear comfortable clothes for this meeting and not bring laptops.

There were formal introductions of our new administrative

staff members, including Ms. Cattlevic and Dr. Winfrey. Opening remarks and the annual pep talk by our superintendent followed. Harriet was very passionate on how important each and every one of us was to the team. I believe a lot of this had to do with the three espressos she had downed prior to heading to work this morning and the second black coffee currently shaking in her right hand.

Harriet continued. "It is my pleasure to begin today's retreat with our special guest, Dr. Ethereal. She will help us explore our inner administrator and find ways to release our daily stress and anxiety into the universe. Each of us today will also receive an autographed copy of her most recent book, *What People Will Believe!* Friends, I give you Dr. Ethereal."

Polite applause followed.

"Welcome, my new friends. It is an honor and privilege to be here with so many eager, intelligent, educated, and dedicated administrators. This is what it is all about!" Dr. Ethereal began.

This, and the two grand the district just pissed away for thirty minutes of theater, I thought. Judging by the looks on everyone else's face, I was guessing they were coming to similar conclusions.

"Our first exercise will focus on trust and concentration. Please get up and form two lines facing each other one arm's length away from the person across from you," Dr. Ethereal said in an enthusiastic, uplifting voice.

All at once, everyone looked down at their phones as if they were receiving an urgent call.

"No, you don't!" Harriet said. "Get up! All of you!"

Busted! We formed two lines facing each other. I was across from Coach Slick. This couldn't be good.

"All right now. A little closer. One arm's length away. For the next thirty seconds, we are going to stand up straight, take in a deep breath, smile, look each other in the eyes, and whistle 'Mary Had a Little Lamb,'" Dr. Ethereal said in a lilting voice.

She's serious! Shoot me now.

Coach was already squirming with his eyes shifting everywhere but where they were supposed to be. I, on the other hand, was trying not to burst out laughing. And it seemed many others were too.

"All right then. We'll start on three. One, two, three!" she counted.

The sound of off-key whistling got as far as the first three notes of "Mary had" when all that could be heard was spitting, snorting, and hysterical laughter! A few attempts to start again made it worse.

"Concentrate and respect each other's focus and fortitude. Have vulnerable moments. We're building trust," she said, trying to pull it all together.

Nope. Not gonna work. She is losing the crowd fast!

"OK, OK, OK," she continued, trying to regain our full attention. "Everyone in the left row, take one step to the right. The end person will go around to the start of the line." Dr. Ethereal was smiling but with a little tension in her voice. "All right. Now greet your new partner."

Oh great! I'm across from Harriet.

Dr. Ethereal continued. "With just facial expressions, try to connect with your partner, and tell them what you think they are trying to tell you, without words. This is how we create emotional connections! Aaaand, go!"

"Whaaaaaa?" could be heard around the group.

Nobody got it! Nobody!

"Don't be shy. Say whatever you think they're trying to tell you with their face," she continued. "Look them straight in the eyes and say … and say … Anyone?" she asked, looking around the room.

This is going well, I thought.

"I think they're trying to tell me it's time for a break," Coach said to the amusement of everyone. Except for maybe Harriet and Dr. Ethereal.

Dr. Ethereal was still trying to smile. But she was sweating.

"All right! I think we're all warmed up now. Take your seats. How are we feeling?" she asked. "Anyone? Dr. Strat?"

I answered, carefully, "I think we are all feeling about the same."

Everyone smiled and nodded in agreement.

"Excellent!" she said.

I was trying to wrap my head around the fact that we were all in the same room yet she was in a different galaxy.

"Our last exercise will cleanse the minds, bodies, and souls," she said confidently. "I would like to begin by having the entire group take cleansing breaths. Now close your eyes and feel yourselves being cleansed. Feel free to shout out the first image that comes to mind while experiencing this exercise."

Crickets …

Dr. Ethereal asked, "Anyone? Your eyes are closed. This is where you can come out of your inner shells. I want you to feel yourselves begin to come free."

She continued, with her eyes closed and voice beginning to crescendo. "Can you feel yourselves coming?"

A little louder and a bit more intense, *"Can you feel yourselves coming?"*

Shouting louder and visibly shaking, *"Can you feel yourselves coming?"*

Her eyes popped open as she stared directly at the group.

This was definitely too much for such a … *mature* group of administrators. The laughter couldn't be stopped. Even Harriet had her head down with both hands shading her eyes while she shook her head and tried to muffle her laughter.

Best two grand ever spent on a guest speaker, my inner voice laughed.

Dr. Ethereal was confused. She asked Harriet if she should finish off now.

I was holding in so much laughter that I was cramping up!

Harriet said, "I would like to thank Dr. Ethereal for coming today. No, that's not what I mean. I ... Let's just take a ten-minute break before our next segment."

Harriet tried to compose herself as she thanked Dr. Ethereal for being here today and escorted her down the hall and to the front entrance.

She tried to keep a straight, dignified face when she arrived back in the conference room. We also gave it our best ... Nope ... Didn't work. One more good outburst of laughter and it was mostly out of our system. But it would never be out of our minds.

Harriet tried to bring the PD back to order. "Our next activity for the day is to break out into groups of three. You're going to write down two facts about yourself and one lie without the other members of your trio seeing what you've written. Your team will then switch your group answers with the group of three to your right. Both teams will then mix all six folded pieces of paper together and try to guess who wrote the note and which of the three answers is the lie."

Since no one was paying attention the first time, Harriet explained it again, followed by "Come on. It'll be fun."

Coach Slick still didn't understand, so we guided him through it.

My group included Mrs. Keller and the middle school assistant principal, Mr. Rogers, who was also new to the district. He grew up in this neighborhood. The group to our left included Ms. Cattlevic, Dr. Winfrey, and Coach Slick.

We wrote down our three answers and put the folded pieces of paper in the center of the table in front of our groups then mixed them up. I was selected to open each paper and read the three statements.

I opened the first paper and read,

"Number 1, I am a second-degree black belt in tae kwon do.

"Number 2, I collect cardigan sweaters.

"Number 3, I was a bomber pilot in the air force."

The six of us looked at each other. Coach Slick guessed Dr. Winfrey. I guessed the new guy, Mr. Rogers. Mr. Rogers raised his hand with a smile and confirmed it was him.

"OK, group, which one is the lie?" I asked.

"Collecting cardigan sweaters!" we all said, almost in unison.

"Mr. Rogers, is it collecting cardigan sweaters?" I asked.

"No," he replied. "I'm not a second-degree black belt."

"You mean you were a bomber pilot?" Coach asked in a surprised voice. "*You?*"

"Yes," Mr. Rogers replied. "And I'm only a first-degree black belt. And it's in jiujitsu."

Coach was visibly shocked. As for the rest of us? Let's just say Mr. Rogers scored an enormous amount of respect points from us.

I then opened the second paper.

"Number 1, I was quarterback for Nevada State University.

"Number 2, I was president of my fraternity.

"Number 3, I'm on my fourth marriage."

We all guessed Coach Slick.

Mrs. Keller said, "Coach, I didn't know you were quarter back in college."

"I wasn't!" he said with a rolling of his eyes.

I said, "You mean you ..."

"Yup, four times," he said. "What can I tell ya'?"

"This is turning out to be quite a day," Dr. Winfrey said.

"Do I dare open another one?" I asked.

"Go for it!" Coach coaxed.

"OK," I said. "Here we go."

"Number 1, I was valedictorian of my graduating class.

"Number 2, I make homemade beer.

"Number 3, I have eighteen tattoos."

There were only four of us left. Dr. Winfrey, Mrs. Keller, Ms. Cattlevic, and me. This seemed to be the hardest one yet. Coach called out me, Mr. Rogers called out Ms. Cattlevic, and Mrs. Keller called out Dr. Winfrey. I called out Mrs. Keller.

The person? ... Reagan!

"You make beer?" I asked. "We need to try some!"

"Nope!" she responded.

"Nope we can't try the beer?" I asked again.

"Nope. I don't make beer," she said.

Coach started, "You mean you have eighteen—"

"All right, all right, listen up. Let's get back around the conference table. Grab a coffee if you'd like then we'll continue with our agenda," Harriet interrupted.

We all gathered back around the table where there were smiles—and some disturbed looks on the faces in this circle.

The next hour was the business portion of the meeting. This included "The New Teacher Evaluation Tool," district goals and objectives for the new school year, state monitoring, our new "School Safety Initiative," and an update of the "Memorandum of Agreement." Most of us woke up when Harriet announced lunch was ready.

The business administrator had this luncheon catered by the Sandwich Wizard Luncheonette down the block. It was made up of deli sandwiches, wraps, salads, chips, sodas, and chocolate chip cookies. You couldn't go wrong with chocolate chip cookies.

It was a pleasant hour of catching up and talking sports, family pictures, arrests, divorces, scandals ... The usual stuff. It was also an opportunity for several board members to make an appearance and pretend they knew who each of us was. They shook hands, schmoozed, grabbed a handful of sandwiches, and then were on their way.

After lunch, we gathered around the table to resume the festivities of this unique administrative retreat. Harriet called the second half of the meeting to order with a reminder that we could not take any food home under penalty of execution.

There was a polite chuckle from the group.

"All right then. We will proceed with today's agenda on legal updates and school mandates. Please welcome our board attorney, Mr. Neverwinn!"

Mr. W. E. Neverwinn had been the board attorney for the last fifty-two years. He was a realty attorney who knew a little school law. More now that his grandchildren showed him how to use YouTube and Google Search. We usually ran things by him as a courtesy, listen, nod, and then "call the State Principals and Supervisors Association Legal Team for the answers." Manda and Gabe were our go-to attorneys there.

Mr. Neverwinn handed out copies of case studies and educational law he got fresh off Wikipedia this morning. He followed up with the 1971 property values in our region through present day. He then began to hand out copies of case studies and educational law again he got fresh off Wikipedia this morning, stopped, stared, then realized he already did that so he told us about the regional property values from 1971 through present day.

"Can't make this stuff up!" Coach whispered to me with a grin.

His nudge and whisper prevented me from falling into a deeper sleep.

"Here are my golden rules for staying out of jail, or at least keeping out of trouble. I know they are true because I got them from real education lawyers!" Mr. Neverwinn joked. But we knew it was true.

"Number 1, don't use the school email or search engines for your personal use.

"Number 2, don't date someone you supervise.

"Number 3, don't friend your students on social media until they are at least twenty-five years old.

"Number 4, always use a Realtor when buying and selling your homes.

"Number 5, never cover your office door windows when anyone is in your office.

"Number 6, never be left alone with a student.

"Number 7, if it's not in writing, it didn't happen.

"Number 8, never drop the f-bomb at work.

"Number 9, it's smarter to be lucky than it's lucky to be smart.

"Number 10, when in doubt, contact the superintendent."

He added, "I may have adjusted one or two of them, but you get the idea. Any questions?"

Coach Slick asked, "If I were to get married yet again, is it legal to marry a student's mother? … Just asking … hypothetically … asking."

The room grew quiet.

"Let's me and you have a little talk another time there, Coach. What do ya' say? Yes?" Mr. Neverwinn suggested.

Coach Slick answered, "Not for me. Ya' know. Just … curious. For a friend."

Harriet quickly transitioned, "Let's all thank Mr. Neverwinn for being here today for our legal updates. We always appreciate it when he stops in."

Mild applause as Mr. Neverwinn gathered his belongings and left.

Mrs. Keller yawned, which started a chain reaction. Even Harriet couldn't hide it.

"All right. I get the hint," Harriet said in an agreeable tone. "Does anyone have anything else they'd like to share for the good of the order?"

The only sounds were papers shuffling, keys being rattled,

chairs being pushed back, and the passage of gas by Coach, who immediately apologized while letting out a devilish chuckle.

"All right then. Let's aim for a smooth opening day and a great school year! I'll be visiting each of your schools on the first day," Harriet said in a pleasant enough voice.

General nodding and mumbling followed as we sprinted for the door. *Another meeting that could have been done by email,* I thought. Then I remembered the guest speaker and changed my mind quickly.

Nah. This was so much better in person, I thought.

CHAPTER 42

Three Rainy Days!

August 17–19, 1964

Today, Monday, was the first of three straight days of rain. Roger, Keith, Micky, Peter, and I had plans to spend the morning in the tree fort trading baseball cards and just hanging out. Tommy had some black paint so we were going to paint the frame on our motorbike when he joined us in the afternoon. Instead, I was stuck home with my brothers and sister.

Mom made us blueberry pancakes and fried bologna for breakfast then turned on the TV. We took our usual spots in the living room to join her.

She let us watch *Captain Kangaroo* instead of her favorite, *The Today Show.* This was followed by *I Love Lucy, Mr. Ed,* then *Jeopardy!* We half watched while falling into a light sleep from time to time. This was getting old fast.

I went back to my bedroom to complete some half-finished airplane models I'd started in June. The glue had an odor I couldn't explain, but I liked it.

When I was finishing up, Mom called us all down for lunch. This was a combination of peanut butter and jelly sandwiches, bologna and cheese, and tuna fish that we devoured instantly.

She was making butterscotch pudding on the stove while talking to one of her many friends with the telephone receiver wedged between her cheek and shoulder. The phone cord was long enough to reach all corners of the kitchen. We hovered around waiting to swipe our fingers in the empty bowl before having some pudding in a dish.

The afternoon began with my mom's daily soap operas. Goose and I snuck out the back door and headed to the corner deli, getting drenched on the way. Once inside, to our surprise, we saw a good fifteen middle schoolers who had the same idea. We spotted Tommy and Keith down by the cupcake racks. They saw us and waved us over. They said they bumped into each other here five minutes ago.

A few high schoolers entered the deli. It was getting more crowded, and the owner was getting nervous. From my perspective, it what a great place to hang out on a rainy day!

The owner shouted across the store, "OK, everyone! Let's start checking out!"

As a few of us headed to the register, one of the high school kids tucked a handful of gum into his pockets while another stuffed a *Playboy* magazine under his shirt.

We paid for some Yankee Doodles, Hostess Cupcakes, and GOOD & PLENTY then headed back out into the rain as the fireworks inside started. All we could see and hear through the window was screaming as the owner slipped on the soaked wooden floor while going after the high schoolers. They ran by us laughing followed by everyone else in the store who didn't want to get in trouble.

Tommy started running toward the baseball fields then turned to join the three of us who were following Keith back to his garage. Well, seven of us all together. We seemed to have picked up a few along the way, and we were all drenched.

Drew, Ashton, and Winston were our age but not in our elementary school.

We grabbed some towels that were in a basket on top of the washing machine against the back wall of the garage and tried to dry off. The rain outside came down harder. We couldn't even see the road so we settled in, sitting on the floor, steps, upside-down buckets, and a toolbox.

We placed our deli purchases in a pile on the top step of the garage that led into the house. Yankee Doodles, Hostess Cupcakes, GOOD & PLENTY, spearmint Life Savers, and two boxes of Tiparillos.

"Whooooooh!" Keith said in a low voice. "We sharing *everything?*"

We all looked at each other, smiling and nodding.

The cupcakes were each split in half, GOOD & PLENTY poured equally into hands, and Tiparillo boxes opened. Drew reached down in his front right pocket and took out four slightly wet matchbooks.

We gathered close enough to the open garage door as we could without getting wetter. The damp matches took a few strikes to light, but we finally got the cigars going. Each of us tried to look cool, even though we weren't sure how to hold them, smoke them, or do anything.

This wasn't too bad. It tasted like cardboard, burning leaves, and my grandfather's den all rolled into a cigar.

Baby puffs looked too ... kiddish. And side of the mouth looked too fake so I centered it between my upper and lower front teeth and wrapped my lips around it. I gripped it with three fingers on top and my thumb underneath. In my mind, I pictured Sean Connery standing tall, distinguished, enjoying his cigar, looking out from his cottage house into the rain. I inhaled hard in anticipation of blowing out a cloud of smoke that would slowly disappear, revealing my manly face and charming grin to be admired by all. Instead, I choked like a cat spitting out a mouse-size hairball.

Tommy stood closer to the rain, giving him that athletic sheen with just enough breeze blowing through his hair as he stared off into the distance.

"Do we inhale them?" Goose asked.

"I dunno," I replied.

"Try!" Keith nudged.

Goose started to puff like he was taking a sip of water every five seconds. He also stared off into the distance, but with a pale face and watery eyes.

Keith wasn't holding his cigar at all. He just let it clench between his teeth as he occasionally gave it a puff.

Our three new garage mates mainly held their cigars at their sides, lifting them occasionally to take a puff as if they'd been doing this since kindergarten.

As we talked about our summer adventures and puffed away, the garage was quickly filling with smoke so we were actually inhaling smoke when we weren't puffing.

Five minutes later the talking stopped. Goose dropped to his knees, crawled out into the rain, and introduced the deli snacks to the driveway. Tommy was next, with me right behind. The cold rain felt good on the back of my neck while I was painting the driveway with the contents of my stomach. When there was nothing left, it kept trying, with no end in sight. The three who brought the Tiparillos pointed at us and laughed … for about twenty seconds before joining us gripping the pavement. We watched our secondhand snacks join together down at the curb.

After a minute or two, and another drenching, we all crawled back into the garage and lay on the concrete floor, some of us facing down, some facing up. Our legs were too wobbly to stand.

Sometime later, Ashton made it to the spearmint Life Savers, cracked the roll in half, threw one into his mouth, and passed both halves around. Taking in deep, slow breaths, the group finally managed to sit up, leaning against the walls of the garage. Ashton, Drew, and Winston made it to their feet first.

"Hey! This was great. We gotta do it again. We'll see you guys around, OK?" Ashton said as if nothing ever happened. Then all three of them made a run for it into the pouring rain.

Keith got up slowly and went into his house after forcing an "I have this under control" smile and a wave.

Goose and I were next. We ran out of the garage and into the rain, stumbling back to the house, getting drenched once again. We saw Tommy pass us trying to find his way home.

Slowly we opened the back door, looked around, then entered the house. We made our way up to our bedrooms while Mom was in the basement doing laundry. I changed into dry clothes and collapsed onto my bed. Once the bed stopped moving, I managed to fall asleep.

A short time later, I woke up when I heard my mom yell dinner was ready. She made rigatoni and meatballs. Goose and I picked but didn't eat much. We later realized Mom didn't even know we'd gone out.

I spent Tuesday, the second rainy day, lying on the couch watching whatever came on the TV next. It was boring, but sometimes boring is good. I considered heading over to the deli again but decided it was too soon to make another appearance. Whenever I looked out the window, all I saw was rain. The entire day dragged on. Maybe I should have built an ark.

It was bedtime when Goose came into my room. TJ and I were talking about the Yankees' chances of making the playoffs. Goose was quiet and just sat down on the floor by the door.

"You OK, Goose? You look bummed out," TJ said.

"Yeah, I'm OK. Just can't sleep is all," Goose said with a shrug.

In my best baby voice, I said, "Do you need a blankie and a dolly, Goose? Goose?"

Goose's eyes and mouth shot wide-open like he saw a ghost. TJ and I just stared.

"What? What did I say? You all right?" I said in rapid succession.

"You're making it worse!" he said on the verge of tears.

"What did he say?" TJ asked in a fascinated kinda way.

Goose began. "I was sitting at the top of the stairs where Mom and Dad couldn't see me. They were watching *The Twilight Zone*. It was about a doll that talked. It was so real. I can't sleep now because I hear noises."

"All right, all right. You can stay here with us for a while until you get tired," TJ said.

We started talking again about the Yankees, but Goose just sat there, looking scared.

Mom shouted upstairs a short time later, "Get to bed!"

Goose got up slowly and went into the bathroom. TJ grabbed my arm and said, "Come on. Hide in his closet."

I slid Goose's closet door open carefully so it wouldn't make any noise as TJ climbed under the bed. Seconds later, Goose came into his room, turned off his lights, and then rolled under the covers.

After moments of silence, it was my turn. I scratched against the inside of the closet door lightly but heard nothing from Goose. I scratched a little louder this time. Goose whimpered slightly. I let a little time go by, just to build the suspense, then ever so slowly began to slide the closet door open.

Goose whimpered louder, but it came out like a broken whisper. "Guys? TJ?"

I slid the door a little more as he whimpered louder this time. "Joey? *Guys? Guys?*"

This was it! I slid the door the rest of the way open and jumped out in the dark. Goose screamed and tried to get out of bed, but just then, TJ Swung his arm out from under the bed and grabbed him. Another bloodcurdling scream as my parents and Dexie ran into Goose's room. By that time, I had already turned the lights back on.

"What happened? What's wrong?" my mother asked, startled by the screaming.

TJ interrupted her immediately and said, "We heard screaming so Joey and I ran in to make sure Goose was all right. Are you OK, Goose?"

Goose stared at us still shaking, but we stared back much more convincingly. He started to say something but changed his mind. He didn't want them to find out about watching *The Twilight Zone*.

Dad asked, "Are you all right now?"

Goose nodded yes but still stared in our direction.

Dad continued. "Well, just call us if you need anything, but your brothers are here. They'll protect you."

Goose's stare turned into immediate eye-rolling.

"We're here for you, Goose!" TJ said in a convincing tone and smile. I just nodded in agreement and grinned.

Mom and Dad tucked Goose back into bed, while TJ and I met back in my room and closed the door. We were laughing as quietly as we could, making fun of the faces Goose was making during the scare. We finally stopped and just lay on the floor with huge grins on our faces.

"Did you see the look on his face when you jumped out of the closet?" TJ finally said.

"And then when you reached up and grabbed him?" I added.

After a few seconds of silence, TJ said, "You have to be ready at all times!"

"Yeah!" I agreed.

There was a loud bang as the closet door swung open followed by a bloodcurdling scream. We jumped, banging into each other and partially losing control of our bodily functions.

"How do you like it?" Dexie said while sneering and pointing at both of us.

Mom and Dad came running up the stairs again and into my room.

"*What now?*" my father said, with that "Enough is enough" face.

Dexie said, while staring us down, "I just came in to check on them. I guess they got scared. Right, guys?"

We both nodded, knowing what Dexie was capable of. Goose was at the doorway giggling a victorious win.

"Everyone! Bed! Now!" my father commanded.

As Mom and Dad went back down the stairs, the four of us acknowledged our wins and losses for the night. But summer wasn't over yet.

I slept late the next day, Wednesday. Well, 9:30 a.m. was late for me. It was the third day of rain, but it seemed to be a lighter rain. Mom asked for volunteers to go to the supermarket with her. By *asked* I mean she told Dexie and me we were going. We were fine with this because it would get us out of the house.

Five minutes later we were running from the front door through the rain to the car. We took the station wagon so Mom could load up the groceries in the way back. Dexie rode shotgun, and I sat behind Mom in a regular car seat for a change.

We pulled into the lot and parked close to the supermarket entrance. We got out of the car and ran through the rain and into the front door.

It was time to select a shopping cart. We selected one that had three out of the four wheels working. The fourth one didn't hit the ground and spun counterclockwise on its own, but it was still the best choice out of the bunch.

We knew school was starting soon, once we entered the supermarket, because the first thing I almost tripped over at the entrance was a huge basket of black-and-white high-top sneakers next to a pile of marble-covered notebooks, fountain pens, pencils, and lunch boxes. Mom let us pick out the square tin box of our choice. I chose the *Voyage to the Bottom of the Sea* lunchbox with a torpedo thermos inside, and Dexie chose the *Petticoat Junction* box. She got Goose an *Addams Family* box, and TJ—well, TJ was in high school now. A plain, brown, paper bag would do the trick.

One of the benefits of going shopping with Mom was that we were allowed to get a huge dill pickle out of the large, wooden barrel. The more it made our mouths pucker, the better it was. Bananas and grapes must be free, because all the little kids sitting in the basket seats were eating them.

Mom began shopping while Dexie and I ran up and down the aisles. Mom would always run into her friends as she shopped, while we brought candy, cereal, and ice cream back to the basket. This, of course, would end with Mom telling us to put everything back.

Five minutes of shopping and we were already bored. Dexie wanted to push the basket, and I wanted to hop in for a ride, almost tipping it over. I hated that I outgrew fitting underneath the bottom of the basket!

At this point, Mom was rethinking her decision to bring us along.

When we rounded the corner to aisle four, Mom saw Aunt Shannon. My stomach immediately tightened, and I was short of breath. I looked around but didn't see Ellen. Just Yeffie. They needed at least two, if not three baskets, to feed their tribe.

The talking and laughing began between the two as the nonadults picked stuff at random off the shelves only to be told to put it back. I wondered if the store was aware that all the snacks kids our age liked were on the bottom shelves and the good stuff that the adults liked were at their eye level. Must have been a coincidence.

I overheard Aunt Shannon tell Mom that the class schedules were being mailed out this week. Another reminder that the freedom of summer was coming to an end.

We went down the aisle with all the cat and dog food and gave our usual rationale as to why we needed a dog. This was when Mom sped up the cart to get to the next aisle, without saying a word.

We all walked together up and down the remaining aisles, stopping briefly at the butcher's counter for chopped meat, hot dogs, chicken, and cold cuts. If you smiled and said hello to the butcher, he would more times than not give you a slice of bologna or cheese.

We finished shopping in just under an hour. It was finally time to leave.

We waited in the checkout line and briefly saw the sun peek through the clouds. This was short-lived as the clouds covered the sky again. We took turns loading the groceries on the belt while the bagger, well ... bagged them.

All of us left the store together walking out to the parking lot and loading the bags into the wagon. We said our goodbyes just as it started to drizzle again.

The ride home was uneventful. Dexie and I just stared out the windows at the rain.

Once home, TJ and Goose joined us bringing the groceries in and placing them on the dining room table.

For the next half hour we knew better than to get in Mom's way as she unbagged the groceries and put them away, keeping the paper bags to use as book covers when school started.

I ran upstairs to my room just to get away. From my bedroom window, I could see Roger across the street coming out of his front door to sit on his porch. It was only drizzling a little so I jumped down the stairs, three at a time, and headed to my Schwinn.

I made the short trip across the street and joined Roger on the porch. We looked up the street and thought the others must be cooped up in their houses so we rode over to our old elementary school to ride around the parking lot.

"What are all the cars doing here? And why are all the lights on in the school?" I asked Roger, knowing he didn't know either.

"Don't know. Let's take a look," he replied.

We rode our bikes up the sidewalk to the classroom to the right of the main entrance. We looked in the window and saw three of our old first grade teachers putting up welcome-back decorations on the bulletin boards and drinking coffee. All three were wearing cutoff shorts, T-shirts with the sleeves cut off, and baseball caps: two Yankees and one Cardinals.

"Ohhh noooo," I said in a bubble-bursting groan. "Is school really going to start soon?"

Roger shook his head, also disappointed. "Guess so."

The teachers looked out the classroom window, smiled enthusiastically at us, and waved.

"Well, that just made it real," Roger said as we waved back with forced smiles.

We hopped on our bikes and pedaled as fast as we could to get the picture out of our minds as soon as possible. Since it wasn't cool to have fenders on our bikes, all the teachers could see through the window was the back of our shirts with lines of mud going up the middle as we raced away. We turned left once we got to the sidewalk not knowing where we were heading, just as long as it wasn't here.

We wound up at the lake. It wasn't open because of the rain so we went in and climbed the ladder to the high diving board where we sat quietly just watching the water—and the summer—going by.

CHAPTER 43

Two Weeks Left and Counting!

August 21

This was a busy week from the word *go*. Monday through Thursday, the team could hardly be seen, having little downtime. Most of the time was spent finalizing schedules, putting together mailings, preparing for their individual portions of the upcoming meetings and orientations, and secretly sending out last-minute resumes.

This pattern was all too familiar to me. Just when I thought I'd seen it all, new craziness presented itself. The only difference was each year seemed to pass by at a faster rate than the year before. I still enjoyed my school community, staff members, and especially helping the students. Yet I found myself enjoying my downtime with family and friends, both at home and at the shore, more and more. There never seemed to be enough hours in the day, or weeks in the year, to do everything I wanted to do or thought that I would have done by now. Just more craziness that fazed me less and less as each year went by.

As I took my daily security lap around the building, I saw the usual signs that August would be coming to an end soon and a new school year would begin.

Coach Slick was running around tending to scrimmages,

busing issues, AD meetings, and equipment distribution and shortages. He was also preparing for the fall sports pep rally.

The office staff fielded students transferring out, new student registration, listening to teacher complaints and minutia, and inputting information on the school "Krappee" program.

Ms. Cattlevic enjoyed technology challenges and had been updating the school web site with Mr. Jopps. From the looks of it, Mr. Jopps was included as a courtesy.

Ms. Frenzy was hip deep in Master Locks trying to assign lockers and locks by grade sections. She was also assisting Coach Slick with gym locker assignments since he was—let's just say—limited in this area.

Mr. Jopps was entering the upcoming freshman class passwords to our network and assigning laptops.

The new catering service was becoming acclimated to the cafeteria and kitchen facility with Iggy assisting.

The marching band left for band camp in the Poconos Monday morning and was due to return Friday. The cheerleading camp was held this week at the local Boys & Girls Club.

The choral director, Mr. Pavarotti, would be in tomorrow to present his recommendations for this year's school musical, holiday tours to the other schools, and choir trip to the Bahamas for board approval.

The student council advisor, Ms. Peppee, had also requested a meeting this Friday to discuss their part in freshman orientation and their promise to the student body of having a Luau once a month in the courtyard followed by a three-day weekend.

The new maintenance department staff had been working on bolting down the picnic tables in the courtyard in an effort to curtail the practice of weekend parties on the school roof.

The guidance department was inundated with student requests to change their schedules based on who they began dating over the summer.

Mrs. Lass would send out the welcome-back letters containing the students' schedules at 2:30 p.m. Friday afternoon. At the bottom of each letter, in bold font and highlighted in yellow, read,

> Changes to student schedules will be made by appointment only. Please contact your guidance counselor. There will be no drop-in meetings prior to opening day.

"Let the magic begin!" Mrs. Lass joked.

I was finalizing the school calendar for faculty meetings, department meetings, administrative meetings, and professional development days.

Throughout the week, random board members would make appearances as shows of support, but mainly to gain access to their kids schedules and to negotiate their locker assignments and parking spots.

When Friday arrived, we were all showing signs of wear and tear. Midmorning, the marching band limped off the buses with several members holding ice packs against their lips; the percussion line had bandages taped to their hands, and the aroma was a telling sign that no showers were had all week. The band parents and director looked as though they had just plowed the back forty in ninety-eight-degree heat. Freshmen were traumatized and seniors earned their look of arrogance.

The end of the day couldn't come soon enough. As office lights were turned off and doors were closed and locked, all I could think about was battling the traffic to get to the shore house. With my car keys in hand, I began to walk out of my office for temporary weekend freedom. At the same time, my honors English teacher, Ms. Savant, entered the main office with a smile on her face and resignation letter in hand.

F@#*!

CHAPTER 44

The Last Full Week of Summer

August 31–September 4, 1964

I slept late again. I guess it was because it was the last full week of summer before school started. I hated to think about going back to school, but in a strange way, I was also looking forward to it. Middle school would be different. At least I knew the janitors.

The mailman came early for a Monday morning. When I got downstairs, Mom was holding a letter from the middle school band director.

"Joey, this is the year you get to decide if you want to play an instrument in the band. Are you interested?" Mom asked.

TJ played the trumpet in middle school band, mostly to go to the spring festival in Atlantic City. He also took private drum lessons, but that didn't pan out. He always wanted to play sports in high school so his dreams of playing like Louis Armstrong would have to be put on hold. He was already going to practices on the freshmen football team.

Dexie played clarinet in the band. She also played violin in the orchestra. She seemed to like it, but I thought she'd give it up too in high school to be on the cheerleader squad.

"Do they have guitars in the band?" I asked.

That reminded me that I never got around to building my own guitar.

"No, I don't think so," she said. "But how about trumpet or saxophone?"

"Maybe trumpet. I could use the one TJ has," I said. "But I still want to play guitar."

"Maybe if you do well on the trumpet, we could talk about getting you guitar lessons," she replied.

"Deal! Trumpet it is!" I said, starting to get my hopes up.

At least I'd get to go to Atlantic City.

My mother opened some more mail while I made my cereal, sugar, and milk breakfast.

"Oh, you and Dexie got your schedules for school," my mother said as she read through them.

My stomach tied in knots. This was it.

"Who did I get?" I said, nervously waiting for an answer.

"Oh good! You have Ms. Obdurate! She's wonderful!" my mother said as she looked up from the schedules.

I almost fell to the floor. "Are you sure? I mean you're not messing with me, right?" I replied with a look of terror on my face.

"Yes, why?" she asked.

Before I said another word, I dropped my bowl of cereal and bolted out the door. I hopped on my bike and made my way to the end of the driveway. My friends were already there. Not a smile on anyone's face.

"I got Ms. Obdurate!" I was almost crying while the words left my mouth.

Roger and Peter got Ms. Obdurate, too, but not Micky and Keith.

"I got some guy, Mr. Stones. Who's he?" Micky said, feeling left out.

"Me too! I guess he's new. At least we could band together," Keith said.

"They're splitting us up!" Roger groaned.

"Well, we change classes in middle school, right? So maybe we'll be in some classes together. Did anyone look at their schedules?" I asked.

All heads looked down, shaking no.

"And all the sixth graders eat lunch together, right?" I asked.

They nodded yes in unison.

"Is anyone going to be in the band?" Peter asked.

I told them I was going to play the trumpet. Peter said he was going to play the trumpet, too, and Keith was going to play saxophone. Roger and Micky were going to sing in the choir.

"Well, we still get to ride to school together. And ... This is b@&*s@$t," I screamed. Hopefully not loud enough for my mother to hear.

"Yeah, b@&*s@$t!" Everyone else agreed.

"One week left," Roger said in an unenthusiastic voice.

We all nodded in agreement then headed to the deli feeling like the end was near. The afternoon was a blur with minimal activities or smiles.

That night at dinner, we talked mainly about school. Dexie liked her schedule. All her friends were in the same classes together, again ... Figured.

TJ had already been going to football practice and getting used to being in high school.

Goose had Mrs. Rollins, who TJ and I both had when we were in third grade. She was all right. A little older than the other teachers. She reminded me of my mother.

Dad said, "Don't forget we have our annual family barbecue on Labor Day. It's always a great way to end the summer. After that, you have one more day to get ready for school."

"We'll be going school-clothes shopping during the week so let me know you plans," Mom said.

"Goose, you should have plenty of hand-me-downs." Mom

smirked, making Goose pout. "But everyone gets some new outfits," she continued, making him perk back up.

I headed to my bedroom after dinner to start my summer reading. It was a hot night so I opened the windows and had my fan on full blast. We had one required reading and one we selected on our own. The required reading was *Where the Red Fern Grows* by Wilson Rawls. I loved reading so I had already read two books on my own since summer started. They were *Animal Farm* and *Adventures of Huckleberry Finn*. So I selected *Adventures of Huckleberry Finn* to report on. Why not get to the good books early on?

Where the Red Fern Grows was only three hundred pages so I finished it that night then fell asleep.

I slept late again Tuesday morning, until almost ten o'clock. After all, it was the last week to get it all in. By the time I dragged myself out of bed, had my cereal, and got dressed, it was almost eleven. It was cooler in the mornings this time of year, and the days were getting just a little bit shorter.

I rode to the end of my driveway and could hear the faint laughter of my friends behind Roger's house in the woods. They were definitely at the tree fort.

"Hey, look who came out of hibernation!" Peter shouted as I entered the realm of the fort.

The others made equally witty jokes as I climbed up the ladder. I rolled my eyes and took it on the chin.

"What are we doin'?" I asked the gang.

"We were thinking of heading over to the lake," Micky answered.

"I'm in!" I agreed.

As we were ready to climb out of the fort, we heard a rustling coming down the trail that separated the backyards and the woods of our road and the next road over. It was Neil and Buzz from the upper numbers.

"Hey! Nice fort!" Neil said in a loud but friendly voice. "Is it cool up there?"

"Yeah, kinda. The trees shade it pretty good," I said.

"Room for two more?" Neil asked.

I looked at my friends who were all nodding their heads yes.

"Sure, but we we're just heading out to the—"

Before I could finish my sentence, Buzz pulled several *Playboy* magazines from under the back of his shirt.

"Yeah, yeah, come on up!" everyone agreed.

Another first. Having the older kids hang out with us, and our first venture into alternate art and literature. Let's just say we entered this venture with an open mind. A level up from *National Geographic.*

We studied, analyzed, and reseated ourselves quite a bit on the fort floor during the viewing, never really making eye contact with one another.

A half hour later, we were all ready to head to the lake and jump into the cold water.

The lake seemed a little more crowded today. The adults with the really little kids were at the shallow section on the left side of the lake by the swings and shade trees. A lot of kids from our grade were hanging out by the swim lanes to the right. We joined them and started to talk with sixth graders from the other two elementary schools, and even seventh and eighth graders. I mean I didn't even know Neil and Buzz were eighth graders. They somehow seemed older. And as we all talked, the gap seemed to get smaller between all of us. Neil and Buzz even introduced us to other eighth graders as their "friends!" And some boys were actually talking to the girls ... and smiling! I don't know why, but for a second, I looked around to see if Ellen was there with her friends.

Nope ... but still ... Every now and then, I would take another look. I guessed going back to school next week wouldn't be so bad after all.

After a really fun afternoon, I headed home for dinner. A new record if anyone had a stopwatch.

Afterward, I jumped up the stairs to my room, still chewing my meatloaf and mashed potatoes, and took my place in front of the fan in my bedroom, making mental notes of names, grades, other kids' schedules, and wondering if Ellen would be in any of my classes. I fell asleep as the sound of the Beatles played on the Hi-Fi downstairs in the living room.

The rest of the week went by fast. At dinner Friday night, we all sat around the table talking about our last week as if next week we'd be going to the stockades. Goose and I had always had a good time hanging together. But somehow, Dexie and I were seeing eye to eye on a lot more things these days.

We finished up dinner with Dad giving us assignments for the weekend to help prepare for Tuesday's Labor Day party. This wouldn't take a lot of time, but Dad wanted us to feel like we were doing this together as a team. He always joked that he should have gone into education because they had summers off to do absolutely nothing.

CHAPTER 45

This Week Was a Nightmare!

August 28–September 1

This week was a nightmare! I thought as I headed home early Friday evening for the extended Labor Day weekend. I debriefed the week's activities in my head over and over again to review what went right and what went not so right. After all these years, some things never changed.

On Monday, August 28, the guidance department phones rang off the hook all day long with student and parent requests to change assigned schedules. Lines were beginning to form at the main entrance, where there was a substantial sign stating there would be no drop-in meetings. Even Coach Slick managed to keep the back gymnasium doors locked.

We held our weekly 10:00 a.m. administrative team meeting in the conference room to go over last-minute details for the week, while watching lines of cars containing disappointed parents and students leaving the parking lot.

The next day, Ms. Cattlevic and our senior class advisor, Mr. Al Symers, were stationed at tables in the main entrance vestibule to welcome and guide our new seniors through the portrait process. Seniors were scheduled beginning 9:00 a.m. and finishing at 2:30 p.m. They each took two picture poses. One with cap and gown and a second with their choice of outfit. The day went as planned with only a few exceptions.

The PTO president brought her entire family in thinking she could get her Christmas card pictures taken today. Mr. Symers convinced her we were on such a tight schedule … Ya' know … She didn't buy it, but they did eventually leave, without her senior daughter who was heading to the courthouse to file papers to divorce her family.

Then the son of one of our current board members, Chad, entered the building proudly displaying two enormous hickeys on each side of his neck. Mr. Symers, thinking Chad would appreciate a little help, offered him makeup the photographer brought in, to hide the hickeys, but Chad insisted they be in the picture. His plan was to add his yearbook senior quote under the picture that would read, "This summer really sucked!"

Being an arrogant youth, Chad would not listen to reason until … Ms. Cattlevic followed him into the auditorium. A few minutes later, his pictures were taken with both hickeys covered. He and Ms. Cattlevic walked back out of the auditorium together. Before he left, Chad promised Ms. Cattlevic a wallet-size picture for her bulletin board. She smiled back at him and said, "See you next week, Chad."

The next day, new staff orientation was held in the media center beginning at 9:00 a.m. Most of the newbies arrived over an hour early. There were doughnuts, bagels, coffee, tea, and water for the twelve of them. I offered the welcoming remarks. Ms. Cattlevic and Coach Slick then began the orientation with the following agenda:

Ave. Ridge High School

Dr. Joseph Strat
Principal
1(225) 189-4751

Ms. Lynn Lass Executive
Administrative Assistant
1(225) 189-4752

Ms. Reagan Cattlevic
Assistant Principal
1(225) 189-4753

New Teacher Orientation

Agenda
August 30

Dr. Strat

- welcome
- overview of academics and extracurricular activities by Ms. Cattlevic
- the athletic program by Coach Slick
- internet use, policies, email assignments by Mr. Jopps

Coffee Break

Ms. Cattlevic

- building procedures, forms, email and internet, grading
- new teacher symposiums
- building tour
- bus tour of the district
- lunch
- afternoon classroom time

Staff Signatures

_____ _____ _____

_____ _____ _____

_____ _____ _____

_____ _____ _____

I joined the group for a bus tour of the district. Quite frankly, I just wanted to get out of the building.

Iggy pulled the bus up to the door by the media center. The twelve new anxious hires got on first, followed by Ms. Cattlevic and Coach. I got on last. Since Iggy had lived in town his entire life, we let him have first shot on the microphone.

"Welcome!" he said gleefully. "For those who don't remember, my name is Iggy. I will be your guide on today's tour. Buckle up, and let's have some fun!"

Our first three passes were by the district elementary schools. This was followed by the middle school and then Iggy's favorite bar. Next we turned down Main Street, where he pointed out thirteen banks, twelve nail salons, and fifteen of his favorite pizza joints. We rode by the municipal building and police station that sat majestically between a Dunkin' and a Starbucks. Throughout, Iggy continued his cruise ship comments. For a town that was four square miles, there was a lot to see.

Iggy turned down a back road by the woods where the hiking trails were but made a sudden left and accelerated to get back onto the main road. The new staff didn't notice anything out of the ordinary, but I spotted three of my high school custodians—who should have been working on the third wing floors—ducking behind a van smoking and enjoying … beverages.

Iggy continued his emcee duties thinking I missed the obvious.

When I scanned the bus, I saw Reagan shaking her head slightly with that knowing grin.

We moved on to the ball fields, churches, parks, and town lake, where a good number of our students were enjoying their last week before school started.

Iggy's final lap around the town showed the most popular places the students partied, the CVS where they hang out, and the railroad tracks and trestle where they got their alcohol and drugs. It was at that moment I grabbed the microphone.

"Any questions?" I asked as we headed back to the high school.

"What's your favorite go-to place, Dr. Strat?" our new physics teacher asked.

"Dunkin' on the way in every morning. As far as lunches go, I rarely get out of the building during the school year. After hours, it's advisable not to be anywhere in town. But if you're going to—let's say—relax with a cocktail, with social media, rumors, and nosey parents, the farther away, the better."

We pulled back into the parking lot and emptied the bus just as lunch was being brought into the media center. There I sat with the new staff members, getting to know them better.

Not a bad group, I thought. *Not bad at all.*

On Thursday, it was the first day back for the district staff members. The agenda began with our superintendent, Harriet, taking the podium. She offered pretty much the same speech as the one on Kumbaya Day to the administrators. The district staff, who were naturally sitting halfway back and off to the sides in the auditorium, applauded with one hand clapping against their cellphones in the other.

Next the board president tripped his way to the podium and said, "Welcome back!" then nodded and left the stage. The PTO president followed up quickly with her pleading for help and passing a basket around the auditorium for donations.

Next on the agenda was a ten-minute video titled *Being a Team Player!* The screen got stuck at first. Then the internet wouldn't sync with YouTube or any Bluetooth device. Suddenly Mr. Jopps entered the stage with arms akimbo and cape draped over his shoulders. The backlighting gave the audience a view of his silhouette. After a reasonable amount of time posing, he got to the business at hand and had the video working in about five minutes. Give or take …

The video might as well have been in black-and-white with

subtitles and ragtime music playing in the background. We didn't know whether to applaud, laugh, stay silent … Anyway, the staff was released to go back to their assigned buildings afterward. Lunch would be on their own.

Following lunch, the staff entered the media center at 1:00 p.m. sharp. Our professional development was delivered by Captain Pike on school safety and security.

"Secure the building at all times!" he began.

He then focused on staff accountability, the necessity to be constantly aware of student, staff, and community safety, the constant updates on state and building protocols, and the relationship between law enforcement and the district through the "Memorandum of Agreement."

As his speech progressed and his passion for the subject grew, a doe and two fawns were walking down the hallway by the media center glass wall for all to see.

"Is this a general lockdown?" a staff member asked the captain.

There was an outburst of laughter, then general … wonder. Why *were* there three deer in the hallway?

"I'll check it out, Dr. Strat!" Iggy assured me.

Iggy went out into the hallway like a champ. Unfortunately, the doe, in an effort to protect her young, hip-checked Iggy into the lockers before he knew what hit him.

"Ooooooooohhhh!" the staff whispered in unison with grimaces on their faces. Iggy got right back up though, and there was thunderous applause.

The deer took off down the hallway with Iggy following steps behind trying to catch up. Coach Slick and Captain Pike followed Iggy. The deer turned left into the main corridor and headed for the gymnasium. The hallway doors were open so the deer entered the gym and ran across the basketball court and out the back door. They had their choice, since all the back doors were open. When Coach and the captain caught up, Iggy was already closing the doors. The three of them looked at each other then looked at the hallway entrance where I was standing, looking directly at Coach with three fingers held up as I mouthed, "Three."

Coach took a second to change his shorts before he met us back at the media center.

Captain Pike picked up where he left off. The staff was still sending out pictures, videos, and emoji on their "private" social media accounts. Then they were even more unengaged than they were at the start of the meeting.

Not two minutes into the training, Mrs. Michelin, a veteran member of the science department, began wheezing uncontrollably. Captain Pike, Coach, and I ran to her table.

"Are there nuts in those cookies?" she gasped. "Allergic … No EpiPen."

Apparently, our new food service included homemade oatmeal cookies with nuts in them for our after-lunch coffee and tea. Captain Pike radioed for an ambulance that arrived less than two minutes later. Our shared nurse was not present at this meeting, but we did have a few EMTs on staff. We gave the staff a fifteen-minute break and escorted them out of the media center.

Once they arrived, the town EMTs had an EpiPen, and soon Ms. Michelin was breathing easier.

"We'll take you to the emergency room just to be safe," the driver of the ambulance said to Mrs. Michelin. "We would have been here a few seconds sooner, but there were three deer standing in the middle of the road."

The room was silent as eyes glanced back and forth at each other.

It was an effort to get the staff back from the break.

The training continued, and Captain Pike received a round of applause. Our last agenda item was to finalize the program for this evening's Back to School Night.

"First of all, is anyone allergic to pizza?" I asked. There were giggles, but …

"There will be ten minutes for each of the eight periods with five minutes in between to get the parents from class to class. The student council will be posted at each corner of the hallways to guide the parents and to answer any of their questions. Work off of the guide sheet Ms. Cattlevic has provided. I will be circulating the hallways, and Ms. Cattlevic and Mrs. Lass will be in the main office distributing schedules to parents if they need them. They will also ring the bell to start and end each period."

"Now pay attention! Your safety word is *wonderful!* If you need help as I pass by, just use *wonderful* in the first sentence. For example, 'Dr. Strat, these *wonderful* parents have a question about …' I will jump in.

"At the end of period 8, I will thank the parents over the PA system then call all staff members to the media center for a debriefing. This will, hopefully, ensure you are not stuck in your room with one or two parents. If they wish, they could set up an appointment with you once the school year begins," I continued.

"What's in the pizza?" a random voice said from the back.

Everyone laughed then went back to their classrooms to finish setting up for the evening and the start of the new school year.

Before the pizza dinner, Mrs. Lass and I were watching the video of Iggy getting hip-checked into the lockers, over, and over, and over again. It was hypnotizing. We even considered sending it in to that *Funniest Home Videos* show.

Can't make this sh%@ up!

The staff slowly worked their way down to the cafeteria for the pizza dinner break. This was a great way to socialize and keep the staff in the building for the Back to School Night. Most staff members stood around and chatted while enjoying several pizza options, while some chose to grab a slice and go back to their classrooms without looking at or speaking to anyone. Every school had them.

Glancing over the room, I remembered my university professor telling the class about staff observations. Not formal observations, but just ... observations in general.

He said, "There are three questions I could ask any administrator, and their mind would go right to the staff member.

"First, who is the one staff member in your school that constantly hangs out in the main office trying to get the latest scoop?

"Second, if there was a report that one of you staff members may be getting too close with a student, who would come to mind first?

"And third, who is the first teacher that comes to mind when you think, *Would I put my own kids in their class?*"

"Keep your eyes and ears open," as Mrs. Lass said.

Following the pizza bonanza, parents, guardians, and staff members filed into the auditorium for the start of Back to School Night. A lot of familiar faces were mixed in with the new.

The first ten minutes went along as planned with everyone taking their seats for the welcome-back pep talk. Harriet, our superintendent, pontificated on the state of the union.

Next the board president stumbled onto the stage wearing an outfit right out of *The Mod Squad* catalogue. His slurred speech was focused on his reelection, what school was like when he was a kid, and how without football, we wouldn't have a school.

He joked, for all to hear, while leaving the stage, "Now that school's starting, the administration will have something to do."

The PTO president was next on the agenda. She questioned why everyone came out for the elementary school PTO meetings, much less for the middle school meetings, and how we might be able to get more than five parents out to the high school meetings.

She finished by letting everyone know how she did everything and how very lucky we were to have her.

I greeted the parents and guardians next. My first order of business was to introduce our new assistant principal, Ms. Cattlevic. Thunderous applause was heard as her reputation proceeded her and had grown over the past two months. I followed up with new staff introductions then yielded the podium to Ms. Cattlevic, who pleasantly guided everyone through the hour and a half of classroom visits. By now approximately 20 percent of the high school parents were in attendance.

The parents were released at the bell and headed toward their children's first-period classes. Those new to the school were guided by the student council members and our faculty.

The evening went along relatively smoothly with only two incidents. There was one parent, who was also a board member, who chose to drop f-bombs in each class they visited as well as the hallways in their not so indoor voice. Another insisted vaping was not smoking and they should be allowed to partake whenever and wherever they wanted. I managed each of these issues without incident.

Prior to the bell ringing, signaling the end of the last period, I thanked everyone over the PA system for attending Back to School Night. Then I called the staff to the media center and guided them out the side door safely to their cars before the parents could find them.

This was it. Friday, September 1, the last day of summer hours. The staff was in today getting ready for Wednesday when the students came back and we started another school year.

I picked up bagels for the custodians and maintenance crew and coffee and bagels for the office staff. Ms. Cattlevic baked cupcakes, and Ms. Frenzy brought everyone a little potted plant for their desk. Coach brought the office staff this year's sporting attire that included shirts and sweatshirts with the school logo surrounded by the phrase "We are Ave Ridge!" Later Coach returned with lined windbreakers for Ms. Cattlevic and me with our names and positions over the left pocket.

I would be looking over resumes for our recent honors English vacancy this morning. There would be a substitute English teacher who was a retired English professor from the county college helping us out until we could find the right candidate.

Captain Pike walked into the main office during the Friday morning festivities. He looked at me, tilted his head toward my office, and asked to speak with me.

This can't be good, I thought. *Then again, maybe it's good news. Right? Maybe I'm getting an award. Maybe I won a raffle! Maybe the lottery! ... ahhh s@&t ...*

I guided Captain Pike into my office and closed the door, knowing Mrs. Lass could still hear everything that was being said.

Captain Pike began. "Uh, last night, after Back to School Night, allegedly ..."

S@&t! ... S@&t! ... "Allegedly" is never a good start! Plus I'm guessing I didn't win the lottery, I thought.

"... your algebra teacher, Mr. Seeplus, plus one of his friends, was arrested later for punching out the board president."

"*What?*" I repeated in a surprised yet impressed voice. "Mr. Seeplus?"

"Plus one of his friends," Captain Pike answered.

"Is it on video or social media yet?" I asked.

"As it was happening," Captain Pike said.

"Did he get 'em good?" I whispered to Pike.

"Wish I were there," he whispered back.

Although none of this was funny ... Come on ... Really?

"Where?" I asked.

"Sloppy Drunk Pub & Grill on Main Street," he responded.

"All that training, in one ear and out the other," I said.

Captain Pike continued. "Seeplus had a few to start his Labor Day weekend early. He walked over to buy Mr. Dumass a drink and accidentally tripped, landing on Mr. president's wife's lap, spilling his drink on her as well as himself. Dumass began to laugh until his wife started licking the spilled drink off of Seeplus's face. Then s@&t got real! Prez pushed him off her and dumped his beer over our math guy's head. He allegedly retaliated by popping Prez in the mouth. His friend did the same in solidarity, and because he was drunk. Prez hit the floor like a sack of—"

"I get the picture," I interrupted.

As Pike left my office, he said, "Oh, by the way, it looks like you have a flat on the front driver's side. Enjoy the weekend, Doc!"

I headed out to my car with Coach and Iggy, who were nice enough to give me a hand changing to my spare tire. Iggy was genuine, while Coach was sucking up trying to earn some points back for the whole keeping-the-building-secure thing. And yes, Pike lent a hand.

I walked back into the main office and saw Mrs. Lass tilting her head toward my office, the same way Captain Pike did.

"What now?" I said to myself while looking up at the ceiling.

I went into my office, where Harriet was already sitting with a cup of coffee. "I poured you a cup," she said, pointing to my desk. "Sit."

I closed the door, sat down, and grabbed my coffee. We looked at each other briefly then couldn't stop laughing.

"Oh, if I could have been a fly on the wall!" she said between laughing.

I choked on my coffee, adding coffee stains to the grease stains already on my shirt from changing my tire.

Once we became adults again, Harriet said, "He's gone, you know ... Seeplus."

"Yeah ... Yeah. And unfortunately, this is media gold," I answered back.

"He'll be put on leave until this plays out, but I believe he will resign first … Shame," Harriet said.

I agreed.

Harriet added, "I may have a temporary replacement for him, but only for a few weeks. Her name is Mrs. Ceenile."

I just gave a dead stare.

We wrapped up our meeting and continued to get ready for opening day next week.

Lunchtime rolled around quickly. Today, we ordered lunch for the staff from our new food service. Nothing special. Just sandwiches and chips. I joined everyone in the cafeteria to catch up on what they did over the summer.

As I was moving from one table to the next, I noticed smoke coming out from the kitchen. The fire alarms blared as staff members scooped up sandwiches and headed out to the parking lot. Iggy, Coach, Ms. Cattlevic, and I ran into the kitchen.

"Grease fire!" Iggy shouted.

The food service manager had already grabbed the fire extinguisher. Seconds later, fire trucks and police sirens were heard in the distance. As they grew closer, Iggy grabbed a second extinguisher and joined in. By the time the emergency teams arrived, the fire had been put out and the kitchen was a disaster!

The emergency crews came in scattering food, equipment, and dead cockroaches onto the floor. Meanwhile, the staff went to the bleachers to enjoy their lunch and take in the freshmen soccer scrimmage. Posts from spectators in the stands were already getting likes on social media. Pictures of teachers eating, talking, and laughing with captions like these:

"The school is burning? Really? The game's not over yet!"

"So this is what teachers do during the summer!"

"Your tax dollars hard at work!"

"School burns as teacher nosh!"

And of course, a female senior saw her young male gym

teacher and gave him a big hug. Caption: "Summer romance! *Are your kids safe?*"

As the emergency team packed up, and the usual, "Thanks for being here for us!" comments were exchanged, Iggy and his crew were working alongside the kitchen staff to begin the laborious task of cleaning up.

The bleacher dwellers were called back in. Their walk back into the building took three times as long as their walk out.

The afternoon went along with some normalcy, other than the large number of seniors driving through the parking lot hoping to see more of a disaster. The bells were set for the new schedule, the PA was tested for morning announcements, and all counters were cleared for the first day of school.

"We're as ready as we're going to be!" I said. "Let's pack up and enjoy the long weekend. Thank you, everyone. You're the best!"

I was going to try my best to relax this weekend. What the heck. It was going to be a great year. ... Yeah, a great year.

But first an end-of-summer drink at Jazzy's with my old friend Tommy.

CHAPTER 46

The Last Weekend of Summer!

September 5–7, 1964

The last week of summer went by way too fast! We did so many things, but it was the weekend. Monday was Labor Day, and school started Wednesday.

Saturday morning was breakfast, cartoons, and getting the house and yard ready for family. Dad cut the lawn with TJ and me following up with the rakes. Mom and Dexie were baking in the kitchen, and Goose was hosing off the lawn chairs and picnic tables.

Once the lawn clippings and late summer fallen leaves were raked to the curb, Dad lit a Kent then threw the match on them. He watched the pile burn while TJ and I poked at the fire with loose sticks.

Goose dragged the hose to the driveway. The four of us washed the cars and hosed each other down in the process. Three of us enjoyed it. Dad? Not so much, but he was a good sport.

Once we dried off, it was time to clean our rooms. I mean if we didn't do it right, Mom would walk through with a garbage pail and throw everything left out of place into it. We learned this the hard way.

For the first time, I found myself deciding what to wear on the first day of school. Normally, it was just jeans and a button-down shirt Mom put out the night before. But this year, going into middle school, I just wanted to look like I belonged there, but just a little bit cooler. I made my selection then began a new book.

Around noon, Mom made fried bologna and cheese sandwiches. I wolfed one down then got on my Schwinn looking for the gang. Everyone was out so I rode by the ball field and saw Tommy looking for a pickup game. No one was really around, and those who were there threw around a football.

Tommy and I played catch for a while. He always brought an extra mitt and bat. Knowing that school started on Wednesday, things kinda looked and felt different. Like the end of ... I don't know. The lake would close after Labor Day, the bases would be put away for the season at the ball field, and the leaves on the trees would begin to turn.

Tommy and I stopped by the deli for Turkish Taffy and Cokes, hung out for a few more minutes on the milk crates against the building in the parking lot, then we each headed home. The days were getting shorter, and the air seemed a little crisper.

I cleaned my Schwinn after dinner, put a few drops of oil on the chain, then rode it up the block to blend it in. Buzz was on his porch and we both waved as I rode by.

This Saturday night was more of a family night. Another clear sign that the summer was coming to an end. We took our spots in the living room. Mom just turned off the Hi-Fi where Elvis was screaming something about a hound dog and turned the Zenith on. My dad had the *TV Guide* so we started with *Outer Limits*. This was followed by *Gilligan's Island*.

Mom let us stay up a little later since it was Saturday and it was still summer. The King Sisters were on *The Hollywood Palace*. Dad wanted to see it; we didn't. But we were too lazy to get up and finally went to bed at ten o'clock. We argued to stay up later, but it was more for show since we were all tired.

Sunday was a pajama and hangout day. No one was around in the neighborhood, and it was cloudy outside. I found myself thinking, *Is it strange that I'm looking forward to going back to school?*

We had a late lunch, and we were all pretty bored. I remember my fourth-grade teacher, Ms. Yaun, telling me once, "Nothing is boring. It just may be uninteresting to you."

Nope. I was bored.

As late afternoon approached, my father announced, in his "the king is speaking" voice, "We are leaving at 6:30 sharp to go to the drive-in movies tonight. We will enjoy hot dogs and popcorn while watching *Viva Las Vegas!* That's right, Elvis Presley and Ann-Margret on the large outdoor screen!"

We all cheered. Not necessarily for the movie but for the hot dogs, popcorn, and pillows and blankets in the way back. Elvis was all right, I guessed, but Ann Margret looked somehow different, better than I remember her looking.

Everyone was ready 6:30 sharp! We loaded up the wagon with all the comfort necessities as well as a Tupperware container of grape Kool-Aid. Dad had a couple of Pabst tucked under the driver's seat, and Mom had a small container of sangria the color of our Kool-Aid in a shopping bag. She thought we didn't notice.

It was a short ride to the drive-in. We pulled in and watched Dad shell out two bucks for the carload. We were there early enough to get a second-row center spot. He drove the wagon up the small incline so we would get a better view of the screen. Not so much from the way back but enough to see most of it. He rolled down the driver's side window, hooked the speaker onto the top, and rolled it back up. It was not quite dark out yet so we were allowed to play on the swings and monkey bars for a while.

When Dad shouted, "Let's go!" we filed in to get some hot

dogs, cheeseburgers, popcorn, and Milk Duds. We worked our way back to the car trying not to drop anything. When we got there, Mom was already halfway through the sangria and smiling that relaxed smile.

The movies began with two cartoons, then the feature film. From what we could see and hear through the window speaker, it was pretty good.

Goose and Dexie fell asleep halfway through. Mom fell asleep next, with a big grin on her face, and TJ and I made it until almost the end.

When I woke up, we were home and went straight to our bedrooms. Dad carried Goose and plopped him down on the mattress. He never budged.

Labor Day!

I woke up early Monday morning. It was Labor Day. Company would arrive around one o'clock so we had some time. Mom served breakfast that included buns, round rolls and butter, and any cereal we still had in the cabinets.

Afterward, we helped set up chairs, picnic tables, and beach blankets. Dad set up his cooking stuff on the brick grill. Earlier in the week, he made another feeble attempt to cement back the bricks he blew off on the Fourth of July. It looked like *maybe* it would hold up until the end of the barbecue.

Dexie was sorting out the forty-fives she would play on the phonograph. Earlier in the week, she picked up the newest forty-five, "House of the Rising Sun" by the Animals, that she placed on top of her ever-growing pile of records.

It was a perfect day for a barbecue with a clear sky and temperature somewhere in the seventies. There was a slight breeze that reminded me of the fall.

At one o'clock our guests began arriving. Everyone from our

camping trip plus our grandparents, a few great uncles and aunts, second cousins, and … Aunt Shannon and Uncle Jessie. This I did not know. They brought Yeffie and Ellen. The older kids in their family were spending the day with their friends and neighbors.

I was avoiding Ellen for some reason at the beginning, but she came right up to me and said, "Hi, Joey! Are you ready for middle school?"

I froze for a moment then gathered enough "cool" to say, "Yeah, I guess so. We still have one more day."

Ellen giggled and lightly punch me on the arm.

I smiled and said, "You wanna see my motorbike?"

"You have a motorbike? Yeah, I want to see it!" she said, apparently impressed.

We walked to the shed, both feeling at ease with each other.

Ellen, Yeffie, Goose, TJ, Dexie, and I hung out together most of the afternoon. Every now and then a great aunt or uncle, who we would only see maybe once a year, would come up and give us all hugs and kisses. Two of the three nuns in the family did the same and said directly to me, "You know, Joey, you would make a good priest."

If they knew me better, they would know there was no chance of that. Everyone laughed with the loudest laughter coming from Ellen. My tanned face took on a reddish glow.

This barbeque seemed a little different. There wasn't so much running around and screaming. Instead, I found myself talking more to my family and guests, especially Ellen. We all enjoyed the afternoon getting to know each other better and listening more to the music Dexie was selecting. Occasionally Goose would get up to go to the swing set or ride his bike up and down the driveway, but once he got it out of his system, he was back with the group.

My brothers, sister, cousins, Yeffie, Ellen, and I took a walk up the block. When we passed the new construction, which was almost complete now, a family with three young kids was walking around the property. We waved at each other and kept walking. When we got to the upper numbers, we ran into Neil, Buzz, and their friends and began to talk about the summer, the motorbike, and the new school year. Surprisingly, my cousins fit right in. We seemed to be merging into one larger neighborhood now rather than the upper and lower numbers. It was like a new chapter was beginning.

On the way back to the house, we saw Mark sitting on the front porch. We smiled and waved as we went by. He seemed like he had always been one of the gang now. Ellen asked me who he was. I told her he was a good friend.

When we got back to the house, Dexie brought up how many new families were moving into the neighborhood. I guessed we didn't realize all the new little kids there were playing on the front lawns during the summer. Ellen said she noticed the same thing in her neighborhood.

I looked over at Micky's house two doors down and saw an army soldier getting out of a car. There were welcome-home banners and balloons on the front porch. Micky ran out of the house crying and jumped into his arms. The rest of the family and relatives followed right behind screaming and crying. We all waved and cheered! Mom and Dad ran to the end of the driveway and joined in cheering.

We walked to the backyard where a short time later, Mom shouted, "Food's ready!"

Just in time. We were all getting hungry.

We ran to the table, grabbing hamburgers, hot dogs, and chicken drumsticks. Once our plates were at capacity, the adults ate at the tables and lawn chairs and the kids settled in on the blankets. Ellen sat right next to me. Dexie saw this and nudged TJ. TJ nudged Goose, who shook his head and rolled his eyes, saying out loud, "Oh brother!"

Ellen giggled. I didn't mind … ya' know … just because.

This day seemed to last longer than any other day this summer. I think it was because everyone was here. The weather was perfect and the background music Dexie was playing sounded great.

For a few seconds, I glanced around at our family then stared off at the trees that outlined all of our neighbors' backyards. If I had one wish, it would be that this day would never end.

We ate, drank, laughed, and joked under a perfectly sunlit summer sky. There was a mild, cool breeze that still blew by every once in a while where you could get a hint of autumn smells as Paul McCartney sang "I Wanna Hold Your Hand" over the speakers of the old phonograph. Ellen looked at me, smiled, then looked down at the ground.

Looking around the blanket, I saw Ellen, TJ, Dexie, Goose, Yeffie, and a few older cousins. This seemed to be a snapshot in time. I wished it could last forever because it just didn't get any better than this. Summer was over, and I was ready to go back to school.

I'd never forget my fifth-grade summer.

CHAPTER 47

Labor Day Weekend

September 2

We used to spend Labor Day weekends down the shore at our beach house. But with traffic on the way back home, the new school year starting, and the risk of never wanting to come back, we had been staying home. We had started a tradition of having our family and friends over on Labor Day for an end-of-the-summer party. Nothing spectacular, just sandwich platters, salads, and a few burgers and dogs on the grill.

Labor Day was Monday so I tried to get some quiet time before the chaos began. While students were preparing what they would wear and how their hair would look for the first day of school, my wife, Ellen (yes, that Ellen) would be throwing away clothes from my closet that were over twenty-five years old and picking out my back-to-school outfit.

I purchased my parents' home when my father passed away twenty-eight years ago. My mom was living in a fifty-five-and-over development across town until seven years ago when we placed her in assisted living the next town over. I visited her often, although her memory was mostly gone. She remembered me and the lyrics to just about any song she had ever heard, but other than that, we talked, laughed, then she forgot. At least she was happy and laughed every day.

Ellen's parents also passed away several years ago. I was still not certain I had ever met all of her brothers and sisters.

This was the third time the neighborhood had turned over since I'd been back. I was the grumpy old man on the porch now. There weren't many kids out playing like the old days. They mostly stayed inside exercising their thumbs and eyes on the computer screen for hours playing video games or getting driven to their friends' houses for playdates … to spend hours playing video games.

The old brick grill my father blew up on that Fourth of July had been replaced many times by my propane grills and smokers that I had relocated onto the back deck that I added years ago. Bicycles and motorbikes were more of a memory of days gone by with only a few exceptions.

The town lake was still up and running, but kids under eighth grade had to be accompanied by an adult now. The baseball fields had expanded with organized town games and adult leagues at night under the lights. Fishing was by permit only.

The woods behind Roger's old house had been cleared and the properties between divided up. I hadn't seen a kid-built tree fort in years. There were monstrous swing sets and built-in pools in many backyards that rarely saw activity. Where dads used to cut their lawns weekly, there were now lawn service trucks lined up throughout the week.

The old deli on the corner was still there. It had been updated with four different owners over the years. Their customers were mostly adults now buying breakfast or lunch, and they had a delivery service that seemed to be most of their business.

The couple who bought Mark's house had invited us over many times and we had done the same in return. About a year ago, they showed us an old, framed picture that was hanging in the basement and asked if we knew anyone in it. Surprisingly, it was a picture of my old friends and me playing Frisbee in the road. It was taken from Mark's living room window. I teared up telling them about Mark and each person in the picture.

My *kidhood* friends had all moved out of town. Most of us kept in touch and some would be here on Labor Day. Tommy never missed a chance to get together.

The weekend flew by, and it was perfect weather for a Labor Day party. Our daughters came over early this morning with their families to help set up for the day's activities.

Mary was a media specialist at our local library, and her husband, George, ran his own mortgage and loan business. They went all through school together in town as friends but really started dating when Mary got back from college. They had four wonderful children: two boys and two girls. There was nothing like the feeling of being grandparents.

Our younger daughter, Ruth, was a researcher where she met Harry after he got out of the air force. They had no children yet, but I understood we may have an additional grandchild soon.

Just knowing your kids were happy made you feel like you did something right.

After some doughnuts and bagels, and a little too much coffee, we all went out on the back deck to pull the tables and chairs together, the same way we used to on our annual camping trips to the Poconos. The beer and white wine were placed in the coolers on ice. Ellen had a special cooler for the grandkids with soda, water bottles, and juice boxes. Our pool was vacuumed and clean, with a stack of beach towels next to the outdoor shower. We were ready to greet our guests.

As one o'clock sounded on my smartwatch, the first guests arrived. They were greeted by our dogs, Smoky and Gypsy, who jumped all over them as if they hadn't seen another human being in years. We purposely had our siblings over at one o'clock and friends at three o'clock. This gave the family a few hours to catch up before everyone else arrived.

The first guests were my brother TJ and his family in a classic 1970 purple Dodge Challenger. Always the fashion plate. He loved classic cars and had never stopped working on engines. But that wasn't the career path he chose. After studying abroad for his bachelor's degree, TJ landed a job at RCA and was part of the team that introduced the Videodisc system in the early 1980s. Today, he was still a partner in a technology conglomerate as a visual arts product designer, book author, and international keynote speaker. He was intense and job focused and could occasionally rub people the wrong way. I just wished he would be himself, relax, and visit a little more often. He was the only older brother I had!

His wife, Brooklyn, was also a successful businesswoman. Honestly, I didn't exactly know what they did so I told people they installed cable TV. Their daughter, Brandy, and son, James, joined us again this year. They worked in the city as freelance designers. James had a girlfriend that he was pretty serious about, whereas Brandy had no time, day or night. She worked like a dog and loved it.

The next guests to arrive were Goose and his family. Goose was now a botanist who traveled the world as an advisor on crop control and botanical survival. His wife's name was Patty, but he affectionately called her Peanut. They had one son who was in his midtwenties, Bud Jr., or as we affectionately labeled him, Little Goose! If you dropped Goose out of a helicopter into the wilderness with nothing but the clothes on his back, he would survive for fifty years—and love every minute of it.

Dexie's family followed. She and her husband had adorable twin daughters, Grace and Ellen. Grace was a veterinarian, and Ellen was a researcher. Dexie was CEO of a sustainable energy company. She met her husband, Guy Wright, in Panama at a self-sustaining village experiment. They worked side by side and argued most of the time. They eventually looked at each other, smiled, and one of them would say, "I win!" The other would usually concede. I'll let you guess who usually won the most. Dexie also put together her favorite songs and Bluetoothed them through my sound system with tunes starting in the 1960s. Once a DJ, always a DJ. The first song that played at random was "The House of the Rising Sun," followed by the Beatles' "Yesterday." Paul was still my mother's favorite, and mine!

Yeffie and his wife, the former Dorothy Pincers, arrived twenty-minutes later. Yeffie studied law, and Dorothy was a medical assistant. Once their only son, Jeremy, graduated with an MBA from our state university, he moved to the outskirts of Pennsylvania and started his own CPA firm. That was when Yeffie and Dorothy became partners in the clothing chain Schultz & Levi. They were mostly figureheads now and spent most of their time on cruises and visiting Disney World.

Most of Ellen and Yeffie's other brothers and sisters were scattered throughout the country. We seldom saw them, but they did occasionally keep in touch on social media, texts, and emails.

We sat around the large rectangular tables and chairs on the back deck, and each cracked open a Pabst Blue Ribbon to toast my dad and Ellen's parents. The next toast was for family and friends who couldn't be with us today. We caught up on all the news, gossip, dirt, and anything else we could share. It was always great to see my brothers and sister together and laughing again. Time went by so quickly.

As three o'clock approached, more guests arrived. Tommy and his wife were first. He brought a couple of mitts and Frisbees just for old times' sake.

Tommy played baseball in high school and in college. Scouts were looking at him pretty seriously until he hurt his pitching arm. He was hit in the head by a line drive ball that knocked him unconscious and landed him at a bad angle on his pitching arm.

I was there when the medical staff tried to revive him. All that could be heard from the pitcher's mound was "Tommy, can you hear me? Tommy, can you see me? Tommy? ... Tommy?"

When he finally opened his eyes, he grabbed his pitching arm and let out a scream. He could never pitch the same again. He was devastated, but with a degree in physical education, health, and driver's ed, he became a high school gym teacher and varsity baseball coach. When he got his master's degree in administration, he became high school vice principal, then principal, and expected to finish his career at his current position as superintendent of schools. I was glad we worked in neighboring districts.

Roger pulled up soon after Tommy arrived. Roger started repairing pinball machines after high school as a part-time job. One thing led to another, and the next thing you knew, he bought into the company. He was a natural. We called him the Wizard. His wife couldn't be here today because she and her girlfriends were on a senior citizens dance team called the Acid Queens, who marched in the Annual Labor Day Parade in the city.

Micky and Keith also couldn't make it this year. At their age, who would have thought they would still be touring with their band? They'd never grow up. And why should they?

Peter and his wife showed up at 3:30. Better late than never! They drove the farthest, from Virginia, where they were both high school teachers. Peter was the high school band director, and his wife, Megan, was a physical education teacher and girls' soccer coach.

So many of our friends had passed over the years. We toasted them, and we were thankful to still be here to celebrate together.

We all sat around the tables talking and sharing memories. Ellen and Dexie brought the food out just as there was an enormous explosion! It was a cherry bomb. Ellen almost dropped the sandwiches all over the deck.

"Damn it, Joey!" she shouted.

I just shrugged and smiled. "Couldn't help myself," I said.

She stared at the crater in the lawn then shot a look back in my direction.

"Oooooooohhhh," everyone said in unison, with smiles on their faces.

Ellen just shook her head and smiled. She was a good sport.

The afternoon quickly turned into early evening as the weather cooled down a bit with a hint of autumn in the air. There was never a lull in the conversations or laughter. I looked around the deck at my family and friends and smiled. It was a snapshot in time, and I was a very, *very* lucky guy.

As the sun started to set, we made our way to the end of the driveway, where we had all met so many times before. We hugged, kissed, and said our goodbyes. I soaked it all in. Ellen, Smoky, Gypsy, and I were the last ones standing as the cars left one by one.

Ellen and I walked to the corner deli for some ice cream. Once we made our selection and were back in the parking lot, she kissed me and giggled. It was just like our first kiss so many years ago. We walked back to our house hand in hand, not saying a word but saying a lot.

CHAPTER 48

The First Day of the New School Year!

September 6

It was the first day of the new school year. Ellen had made breakfast as I relearned how to tie a tie. I put on the new clothes she laid out for me the night before. Interesting to note, before we were married, I used to know how to dress myself. Once married, it was apparent I didn't.

Ellen walked me to the front door, and after a long hug and a kiss, then a nod followed by a knowing glance, I was on my way.

I wanted to get to the building early, but Ms. Cattlevic and Mrs. Lass still beat me in. We were ready. The staff was dressed professionally, and the students entered in all their sartorial splendor. Even Iggy put on a clean shirt for the occasion. I barely recognized him.

At the first bell, the students cleared the hallways to go to their period 1 classes. A few new students were holding their schedules not knowing which way to go, so upperclassmen helped them, along with my administrative team. Two minutes later, the second bell rang.

For the first fifteen minutes, teachers took attendance,

distributed locker assignments, locks, and lanyards, and went over *The Student/Parent Handbook* app. You could see both the students and teachers were happy to be back together with their friends and classmates again. It was a new school year and a fresh start for everyone.

At the next bell, the students were guided down to the auditorium for our welcome-back assembly.

Students sat by class. Seniors up front, juniors behind them, sophomores to the left, and freshmen to the right. The new student council president stepped up to the podium to lead the school in the pledge to the flag.

Once the students and staff were seated, I approached the podium for the welcome-back address. This would be my last. I would be retiring at the end of the school year.

I slowly looked around the auditorium and saw the future: eager and enthusiastic students and teachers excelling in the academics, athletics, and the arts.

The last person I set my eyes on was Ms. Cattlevic. She was seated to the left of me on stage. I smiled as she winked at me and gave a thumbs up. The school would be in good hands.

It was a good run, and I'd been very fortunate to meet so many wonderful people throughout the years. We all made a difference in each other's life.

Ellen and I would finally get to open a small cafe and bookstore. We would travel, relax at the beach house, and get acclimated to our new life together. This was the natural course of things.

But before all that, I would like to have just one more fifth-grade summer.

Printed in the United States
by Baker & Taylor Publisher Services